SHOWDOWN!

There was a soft step.

Jerry looked and saw a man with black hair and a pair of shiny black eyes standing in the doorway.

Beyond a shadow of a doubt, this was the man he was looking for.

"Langley!" called Jerry and came out into the open.

His own hand was hanging in midair, ready for the lightning reach of his gun; but the black-haired master of the house turned without haste and faced him.

"Get out your gun," said Jerry, keeping his voice soft. "I'm here for you."

Langley smiled.

WARNER BOOKS By
MAX BRAND

GUNMEN'S FEUD

Max Brand

WARNER BOOKS

A Warner Communications Company

Originally published in 1920 in *Western Story Magazine* as
JERRY PEYTON'S NOTCHED INHERITANCE,
written under the name of David Manning.

This Warner Books Edition is published by arrangement with
Dodd, Mead & Company,
79 Madison Avenue,
New York, N.Y. 10016

Warner Books, Inc.
666 Fifth Avenue,
New York, N.Y. 10103

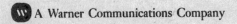 A Warner Communications Company

Printed in the United States of America

First Warner Books Printing: *April, 1984*

10 9 8 7 6 5 4 3 2 1

GUNMEN'S
FEUD

I

When the doctor told Hank Peyton that he was about to die, Hank took another drink and closed the secret inside his thin lips; but when, on the third morning following, he fell back on his bed in a swoon after pulling on his boots, Hank lay for a long time looking at the dirty boards of the ceiling until his brain cleared. Then he called for his tall son and said: "Jeremiah, I'm about to kick out."

Jerry Peyton was as full of affection as any youth in the town of Sloan, but the regime of his father had so far schooled him in restraining his emotions that now he lighted a match and a cigarette and inhaled the first puff before he answered: "What's wrong?"

"That's my concern and not yours," the father said truthfully. "Further'n that, I didn't call you in here for an opinion. The doctor give me that three days ago, Jeremiah." He always pronounced the name in full; he characteristically despised the nickname which the rest of the world had given to his son. "I got you here to look you over."

He was as good as his word, but the only place he looked was straight between the eyes of Jerry. At length he sighed and turned his glance back to the ceiling, a direction which never changed while he lived. "I'm about to kick out," went on the father, "and bringing you up is about all the good I've done, and, take it all around, I'm satisfied."

After a moment of thought he said to the ceiling: "You ain't pretty, but you can ride straight up. Answer me!"

"Yes," said Jerry.

"You talk straight."

"Yes."

"You shoot straight."

"Some say I do."

"You got a good education."

"Fair enough. But not too good."

"Ain't you got a diploma from the high school?"

"Yes."

"Then don't talk back. I say you're educated and mostly I run this roost. What?"

"Yes," Jerry replied.

"I leave you a house to live in and enough cows to grow into a real bunch—if you work. Will you work?"

"Is this a promise you want?" asked Jerry, troubled.

"No."

"Well, I'll try to work."

"I leave you one thing more." He fumbled under the bedding and drew out a revolver. "You know what that is?"

"The Mexicans call it the Voice of La Paloma."

"They call it right. You take that gun. Before you die

you'll hear men say a lot of things about your pa—and mostly they'll be right; but afterwards you go home and pull out this old gun and say to yourself: 'He was a crook; he was a hard one; but he had plenty of grit, and he done for La Paloma that made the rest take water.' "

"I shall," said Jerry.

After a time the father said: "Look at my legs."

"Yes."

"The boots?"

"They're on."

"Good," said Hank Peyton. He added a moment later: "How do I look?"

"Like you'd hit the end of your rope."

"You lie," said Hank, "I can still see the knot in the ceiling." And forthwith he died.

When he was buried, the old inhabitants of Sloan said: "Who would of thought Hank Peyton would die in bed?" And the new inhabitants, who were the majority, added: "One ruffian the less."

Around Sloan, the government had built a great dam to the north and irrigation ditches were beginning to spread a shining, regular pattern across the desert. Very few of the cowmen took advantage of all the opportunities which water threw in their way; but a swarm of newcomers edged in among them and cut up the irrigation districts into pitiful little patches of green which no true cattleman could help despising; the shacks of Sloan gave way to a prim, brick-fronted row of stores; the new citizens elected improvement boards; they began to boost.

Very soon Sloan was extended in all directions by a checkering of graded streets and blocks which the optimists watched in confident expectation. But old-timers were worried by floors so cleanly painted that spurs could not be stuck into them when one sat down; they scorned, silently, the stern industry and sharpness of the homemakers; and many a cowpuncher was known to ride up the main street, look wistfully about him, and then without dismounting turn back toward his distant bunkhouse; for of the many faces of civilization, two were turned to each other eye to eye in Sloan, and the differences were too great for composition.

For instance, among the cattlemen, law was an interesting legend which in workaday life was quite supplanted by unwritten customs; among the farmers and shopkeepers of Sloan, law was an ally or an enemy as the case might be, but always a sacred thing. From that point of view, Hank Peyton was one of the most fallen of the profane, and therefore the townsfolk drew a breath of relief when they heard of his death.

It cannot be said that even the cowpunchers grieved very heartily; but they respected at least certain parts of his character, and above all they had an abiding affection for his son, Jerry. For his sake they were both sorry and glad, and it was generally understood among them that when his father was out of the way, Jeremiah Peyton would shake up the old Peyton place and put it abreast of the times. They waited in vain for the signs of uplift. Jerry was willing enough to talk over changes and improvements with the wiser and more experienced heads among his neighbors, but when it came to tactics of labor he failed miserably, no matter how excellent his strategy of planning might be.

Sheriff Sturgis, who was the only county official to retain his place in the new regime, said: "The trouble with Jerry is that his dad sent him away to school for just long enough to spoil any likin' for work he might of had; but he didn't stay in school long enough to learn a way of sittin' down and makin' a livin'."

This was the general opinion, for after the death of Hank Peyton, Jerry drifted along in his usual amiable manner. He made enough busting broncos in the round-up seasons to see him through the remainder of the year in idleness, and he picked up from his little bunch of cows a few bits of spending money. The cowmen excused him for virtues of courage and generosity, but the townsfolk saw only the black side of the picture, and in their eyes Jerry was "plain lazy."

They waited for the latent fierceness of his lawbreaking father to appear as the fortunes of the son declined month after month. His personal appearance remained as prosperous as ever, but the townsfolk noted with venomous pleasure that his little string of horses was gradually sold off until he retained only a few cow-hocked, knock-kneed mustangs, and one buckskin mare with the heart of a lion and the temper of a demon.

It may be gathered that, by this time, Jerry had reached a point of argument between cowpuncher and farmer. The one faction held that he retained the buckskin because he loved her; the farmers were certain that he kept her only because of her viciousness and the fights which it gave him.

In truth, they could not understand him. Jerry was a tall, gaunt man with heavy shoulders, a pair of straight gray eyes, and a disarming smile; he was, indeed, a mass of contradictions. When he sat in silence he had an ugly, cold look; when he was animated he was positively handsome. The cowmen understood him hardly more than the farmers, but they had faith, which levels mountains.

All this time Jerry may have known that he was

frequently the subject of conversation, though none, even of his closest friends, had courage enough to tell him what was said; but whatever he knew, Jerry was content to drift along from day to day, sitting ten hours at a time on his front veranda, or riding to town and back on the buckskin.

From time to time the danger of approaching bankruptcy stood up and looked him in the face; but he was always able to blink the thought away—and go on whistling. Only this thing grew vaguely in him—a discontent with his life as it was, a subtle displeasure which was directed not against men but against fate, a feeling that he was imprisoned. In the other days he had always thought that it was the stern control of his father which gave him that shackled sensation, but now the first of the month, and its bills, was as dreaded as ever was any interview with terrible Henry Peyton, drunk or sober. He was not a thoughtful man. Sometimes his revolt was expressed in a sudden saddling of the buckskin mare and a wild ride which had no destination; more often he would sit and finger the Voice of La Paloma.

It was an odd name for a revolver, for La Paloma means the dove; but there was a story connected with the name. Once upon a time—and after all it was not so long before—a little man with a gentle voice came to Sloan, and because of his voice the Mexicans called him La Paloma. He was an extremely silent man; he hardly ever spoke, and he never argued. So that when trouble came his way he put his back to the wall and pulled his gun. In a crisis the first explosion of his gun was his first word of answer, and eventually the imaginative Mexicans called the weapon the Voice of La Paloma.

After a time the reputation of La Paloma followed

him to Sloan from other places. A federal marshal raised a posse to find the little man. They found him but they did not bring him back, and with that a wild time began around Sloan, in which the officers of the law figured as hawks, and La Paloma was a dove who flew higher still and knew how to swoop from a distance and strike, and make off with his gains unharmed. He kept it up for months and months until Hank Peyton crossed him.

There was an ugly side to the story, of how Peyton double-crossed the outlaw, after worming his way into La Paloma's confidence, and sold him to the federal marshal. Be that as it may, the bandit learned the truth before the posse arrived and started a single-handed fight with Jerry's father. When the marshal arrived, he found Peyton in the cabin, shot to pieces, but with the gun of La Paloma in his hand, and the bandit dead on the floor.

It was small wonder that that story kept running through Jerry's head day by day as his inheritance melted through his prodigal, shiftless fingers. Before long, little would remain except the Voice of La Paloma, and whenever Jerry thought of that time of destitution he looked at the revolver and remembered the carefree life of La Paloma; there were no shackles on his existence. His commission to a free life was this little weapon, and for a signature of authority it bore eleven notches, neatly filed.

2

The crisis drew near in Jerry's life; the people of Sloan almost held their breath while they watched developments. The mortgages on the old Peyton place were to be foreclosed and neither man, woman, nor child in the town expected the son of Hank Peyton to look quietly on while the land and the house changed hands. The men who held the mortgages had lawyers for agents; the lawyers had Sheriff Sturgis; Sheriff Sturgis had a posse of good men and true at his call; yet for all that, he was observed to wear a look of concern. The sheriff was not a student, but he had a natural belief in inherited characteristics, and he had known Hank Peyton when Hank was in his prime. Nevertheless, the storm broke from an unexpected quarter.

Jan van Zandt held one of the outlying alfalfa farms near the Peyton place, and one day he found Jerry's buckskin mare lying with a broken leg in his largest irrigation ditch; she had come through a rough place in his fence and slipped on a concrete culvert. Jan van Zandt sent a farmhand to tell the tidings to young Peyton; in the meantime he got on his fastest horse, made a round of his neighbors, and returned with a dozen men at his back. They sat down with shotguns and rifles near at hand to wait for Jerry.

He came alone and he came on foot, for there was nothing on his place except the buckskin that he deigned to ride. At first he paid no attention to the men, but sat for a long time holding the head of the patient, suffering horse before he shot her through the temple; only then did he turn to Jan van Zandt.

Jan stood with a double-barreled shotgun in both big hands, and from a distance he kept shouting that he knew he was to blame for letting the fence fall into disrepair, and that he would settle whatever costs the law allowed.

"You fool, do you think your money can buy me another Nelly?" Jerry asked.

Then he went to Jan van Zandt, took the shotgun out of the big hands, and beat the farmer until he was hardly recognizable. The friends of van Zandt stood by with their guns firmly grasped but they did not fire because, as they explained later, they might have hurt Jan by mistake.

Afterward Jerry refused to bring suit for the value of his horse; but as soon as Jan was out of bed he filed a suit for damages in a case of assault, and he won the suit. The cowpunchers rode in singly and in pairs to Jerry and offered their assistance against the "dirty groundhogs," but Jerry turned them away. He sold most of the furniture in his house and the rest of the horses to pay the fine; but with the money he sent a note to Jan van Zandt warning him fairly that Nelly was still unpaid for and that in due time he, Jeremiah Peyton, would extract full payment; he only waited until he discovered how such a payment could be made.

It was another occasion for Jan van Zandt to mount his fastest horse—he was quite a fancier of fine breeds— and this time he rode straight into the town of Sloan, thrust Jerry's note in front of the sheriff, and demanded police protection.

The sheriff was a fat, shapeless man, with a broken nose, little, uneasy eyes, and a forehead which sloped back and was immediately lost under a coarse mop of hair. His neck was put on his round shoulders at an angle of forty-five degrees, and as he was continually glancing from side to side he gave the impression of a man ducking danger, or about to duck. It was strange to see big Jan van Zandt lean over the desk and appeal to this man, and of the two, the sheriff seemed by far the more frightened. His twinkling, animal eyes looked everywhere except at Jan van Zandt until the story was over.

Then he said: "You got some fine horses out there, haven't you, Jan?"

"The best in the country," Jan replied readily, "and if you pull me through this you can take your pick."

"You got me all wrong," the sheriff said. "I don't want any of your hosses. But if I was you I'd not feel safe even if I had six men with guns around me day and night. I'd get on my fastest hoss and hit straight off away from Sloan."

The big man turned pale, but it was partly from anger. "Are you the sheriff of this county, or ain't you?" he asked.

"Just now," answered the sheriff, grinning, "I wish to heaven that I wasn't."

From anyone else that speech would have been a damaging remark, but the record of the sheriff was so very long and so very straight that not even the farmers of Sloan had dared to think of displacing him. He was a landmark, like the old Spanish church in Sloan, and his towering reputation kept the gunmen and wrong-doers far from the town. The admission of Sturgis that he feared young Peyton therefore made Jan van Zandt set his jaw and stare.

"You want me to move?" he said at length. "You want me to give up my home?"

The sheriff looked at him curiously. Sturgis was not accustomed to these homemakers, as yet; but he dimly realized that Jan van Zandt's hearth was his altar and that he would as soon renounce his God as leave his house.

"I don't want you to give up nothin'," the sheriff said. "I want you to take a vacation and beat it off. Stay away three months; and before the end of that time Jerry will be gone—the only thing that keeps him here now is you."

"Go away," repeated Jan van Zandt huskily, "and leave my wife and my girls out there—alone?"

"Good heavens, man!" burst out Sheriff Sturgis. "D'you think Jerry Peyton would lay a hand on your women-folk? I tell you, van Zandt, the boy is clean—as my gun!"

"He's a bad man," Jan van Zandt solemnly said. "Sheriff, I've seen him as close as I see you now, and I've seen him worked up."

The sheriff noted the black and blue patches on the face of van Zandt, but he said nothing.

"He's bad all through, and when a man is crooked in one thing he's crooked in everything."

"Listen to me," the sheriff said. "I've lived—"

"Right's right," interrupted van Zandt stubbornly. "One bad apple'll spoil a whole barrel of good ones. That's true, I guess, and if it's true, then if there was ever any good in Peyton the bad has turned him all rotten long ago."

Sturgis looked at the pale, set face of the farmer with a sort of horror. He felt tongue-tied, as when he argued with his wife on certain subjects; and all in a breath he hated the narrow mind of van Zandt which used maxims in place of thought, and at the same time he respected a man who was determined to stay by his home even if he had to die there.

The little, bright eyes of the sheriff looked out of the window and followed a rolling, pungent cloud of dust down the street; in the narrow mind of the farmer he had caught a glimpse of certain rocklike qualities on which a nation can build. He sprang to his feet and banged his fist on the desk.

"Get out of here and back to your home," he said. "I've seen enough of your face. Peyton says he expects payment for his mare, does he? Well, he has a payment coming to him, I guess!"

"I'll give him what the law grants him," said van Zandt, backing toward the door but still stolid.

"Aw, man, man!" groaned Sturgis. "You come out of smooth country and smooth people. What kind of laws are you goin' to fit to a country like this?" He waved through the windows toward the ragged mountains which lifted to the east of Sloan Valley.

Jan van Zandt blinked, but he said nothing and he

thought nothing; he saw no relation between law and geology.

"Go back to your home," repeated the sheriff. "How do I know Peyton is going to try to harm you? I'm here to punish crimes, not read minds. Get on your way! What do I know about Peyton?"

"You told me yourself that if you was in my place—"

"But I ain't in your place, am I? What a man thinks don't count on a witness stand, does it? Legally, I know Peyton is a law-abidin' citizen."

"Sheriff Sturgis," said the farmer sternly, "leastways I've learned something out of this talk with you. You call him law-abidin'? I know he's young, but he has a record as long as my arm. D'you deny that?"

The sheriff swallowed. "Gunslingers don't count," he said. "S'long, van Zandt."

Sturgis stood at the window, scowling, and watched the big farmer mount his horse. It was a chestnut stallion, a full sixteen hands tall, clean limbed, straight rumped, with a long neck that promised a mighty stride. He made a fine picture, but what good would he be, thought the sheriff, in a twenty-four-hour march across the mountains? Or how would those long legs, muscled for speed alone, stand up under the jerking, twisting, weaving labor of a roundup. The chestnut was a picture horse, decided the sheriff, made for pleasure and short easy rides, together with a long price.

Jan van Zandt disappeared down the street, borne at a long, rocking gallop, and the sheriff turned his glance to his own little pinto, standing untethered, with the reins thrown over his head. The pinto had raised his lumpish head a trifle and opened one eye when the stallion started away with a snort; then he dropped back into his sullen slumber, his ears flopping awry, his lower lip pendent, one hip sagging.

The pinto was six, but he looked sixteen; he appeared about to sink into the dust, but if a choice was to be made between that pinto and the chestnut stallion for a sixty-mile ride the sheriff would not have hesitated for a second in making his decision. He was so moved as he thought of these things, that he leaned out of the window and cursed the mustang in a terrible voice, and the pinto raised his head and whinnied softly.

3

Three days went slowly, slowly over the head of the sheriff. During that time he was as profane, as slovenly, as smiling as ever, and yet every minute he waited for the crash. His mind reverted to a period fifteen years before when Hank Peyton had been a black name around Sloan. There were two men of might in those days—Peyton and La Paloma—and only by an act of grace was Sloan rid of them when Peyton killed the more famous bad man and was himself so terribly shot up that he could never draw a weapon again with a sure hand.

After that epic battle he had lived on his savage reputation alone, peacefully; but the picture in the sheriff's eye was the old Hank Peyton. Side by side with it he saw the son of the gunfighter, equally large, stronger, cleverer, and possessing one great attribute which his father had never known—a sense of humor.

Hank had been all fire, all passion, but his son knew how to smile and wait—in fact, the sheriff knew that he was waiting even now to take the life of Jan van Zandt, and the suspense of that expectation was more terrible to him than the most violent outrage Hank himself had ever committed.

Looking into the future, the sheriff found himself already accepting the death of Jan van Zandt as an accomplished fact, and his concern was wholly for his own troubles when he should have to take the trail of young Peyton; but sometimes a sinister, small hope was mixed with his worry—a hope that Peyton was waiting so that he could make his kill with impunity. After all, that was the only satisfactory explanation of the long wait.

It was on the third day that the unexpected blow fell. Six men rode into Sloan. They raced their horses straight to the office of the sheriff, and, looking out of the window, he smiled when he saw the horses mill about as soon as the masters dismounted. They had saved two minutes by racing, he saw, and now they wasted an equal amount of time tethering their nervous horses; for they rode the type of horseflesh that Jan van Zandt rode—blooded fellows with which they hoped to build up a fine stock for saddle and harness.

"New horses, new men," decided the sheriff calmly, as he recognized Rex Houlahan, Pete Goodwin, Gus Saunders, Pierre la Roche, and Eric Jensen.

He had just about decided that the blow had fallen, when he saw the hulking form of Jan van Zandt himself in the background, and never was sight more welcome to the sheriff. The six men came for his door in a bunch, wedged in the frame, and struggled for a moment before they sprawled into the room. It gave the sheriff time to finish working off an ample chew of Virginia tobacco, for which he was duly grateful.

"It's happened," said Pete Goodwin.

"He's up and done it," said Rex Houlahan.

"The thing, it is finish," said Pierre la Roche.

They said these things all in one breath; the sheriff turned and blinked at Jan van Zandt to make sure that he was not a ghost. But he hated to ask questions, so he said nothing.

Van Zandt worked his way to the front, and Sheriff Sturgis saw in his face the pallor of a coward cornered or a peaceful man with his back to the wall and ready to fight. He had never seen another man who looked exactly like that and it troubled him.

"Prince Harry," began the big farmer, and then stood with his mouth working while the sheriff wondered what on earth the chestnut stallion's name could have to do with six armed men, "Prince Harry," continued van Zandt, exploding, "the skunk has got him—and I'm going to get his hide! Peyton got him—Prince Harry."

"Killed him?" asked the sheriff, seeing light.

"Stole him. There's a law around here about hoss thieves, ain't there? Well, we're here to use it!"

"Young Peyton has a rope comin' to him," added Houlahan, "and we're here to use it."

"There's a law about horse thieves," admitted the sheriff with grim satisfaction, "but it ain't a written law."

There was a chorus of disapproval. It reminded the sheriff that there is one power more terrible and blind and remorseless than the worst gang of outlaws that ever raided a town, and that is a number of peaceful, law-abiding citizens who rise en masse for their rights. The sheriff lost all desire to smile.

"Gents," he said, "if I was to see with my own eyes young Peyton climbin' on the back of another man's hoss, I'd disbelieve my own eyes. Hoss stealin' ain't up to his size. That's all."

Big van Zandt leaned over the desk, resting his balled fists upon it. "How d'you know?" he said. "Seems to me like you're too fond of this Peyton!"

"I got to ask you to take your hands off'n my desk," said the sheriff coldly. "You'll be messin' up all my papers pretty soon."

In spite of his rage, van Zandt knew enough to obey.

"Who saw Peyton take the chestnut?" went on the sheriff.

"Who else would take him?" asked six voices, and the sheriff gave up all attempt to reason with them.

"Even if he ain't got the horse now," van Zandt said, "it only shows that he's passed Prince Harry along the line to some of his friends in the hills. It ain't the first hoss that's been lost around here—and the others have gone the same way. Besides, where does Peyton get all the money he blows in around town? We have to work; he don't do a tap. I ask you, what does that mean?"

The sheriff looked into each face in turn and saw that he could not answer. He only said: "Boys, you may be right. I hope you ain't, but you may be right."

There was a deep-throated growl in response, but they were somewhat pacified by this admission.

"I ask you to do this," the sheriff continued. "Take the road down the valley and try to ride down the gent that took Prince Harry."

"They ain't a hoss in the valley that could catch him," said van Zandt with gloomy pride.

"I got some money that would talk on that point,"

said the sheriff calmly. "But all I say is: Will you do what I want?"

"We'll go down the valley," said Houlahan, combing his red beard. "But who'll go up the valley? We got six here to go down the valley, but where's six to go the other way?"

"I'll go," said the sheriff, buckling on his belt.

Their breath of silence admitted that it was a sufficient answer. "And if neither of us get him?" they asked.

"Then," sighed the sheriff, "it's up to me to hit the trail. We'll start botherin' about that when the time comes. Now you better be gettin' on your way."

"But what if Prince Harry was taken across the hills?"

"Nobody but a fool would take that hoss through the hills," said the sheriff sharply. "He'd bust his skinny legs in the rocks inside of two mile. Now, get on your way."

He followed them through the door, watched them tumble into the saddle and race down the street, shouting. Then the sheriff climbed into the saddle on his pinto. He used neither spurs nor quirt to start his mustang into a racing gait, but the pinto, as soon as the reins were drawn taut, broke from a standing start into a long, lazy lope, unhurried, smooth as the rocking of a ground swell. His head hung low, his leg muscles were relaxed, he seemed to fall along the ground, and he could keep close to that pace from sunrise to sunset.

Sheriff Sturgis paid no attention to his surroundings for some distance out of town. He was thinking of the man who took Prince Harry; if he were a man wise in horseflesh, he would keep far from the hills and go straight along the road. The chances were large that he would give his horse the rein for some distance out of the environs of the town; in fact, he would go at full speed until he had passed the forking of the roads, far up the valley—if he were traveling in that direction.

Once there, he would be in sparsely filled range land where there were no houses within a day's ride ahead of him; and also where he would have small chance of getting a fresh mount. Realizing this, if he were at all familiar with the country, the thief would dismount and let his horse get his wind, preparing for the long grind through the foothills; but after the pause there was a great chance that the chestnut, winded by the hard riding and soft from the sort of work which Jan van Zandt gave him, would be stiff and almost broken down. The greatest difficulty before the sheriff was to decide on which of the roads the criminal would follow when he reached the forking. That is, granted that he took this direction up the valley.

His last doubt was presently removed from his mind, for coming to a stretch of road where the prints of horses' feet were few, and these only the tracks which followed squarely between the wheel ruts, the sheriff discovered new signs that made him dismount from his horse to examine them more closely.

What he found was the print which a horse makes when it runs at full speed, the feet falling in four distinct beats, at about an equal distance from one another, and then a long gap where the last hoof leaves the ground and the body of the animal is thrown forward through the air.

The sheriff watched these tracks with painful attention, and then, to settle any remaining doubts, he got into the saddle on his pinto and spurred him into a hundred-yard sprint. At the end of it, he reined in the mustang and dismounted again. There were now two parallel tracks of running horses, but the differences between them were great.

The first comer outstrode the pinto by an astonishing distance, and in spite of the fact that the wind had drifted a good deal of sand into the marks, the indentations of the other horse were much deeper. It was the track, indeed, not of a cattle pony, but of a heavy horse which had enough blood to get into a racing stride; it was the track of a long-legged animal, and the mind of the sheriff reverted at once to the picture of Prince Harry and his long neck, a sign of speed.

Before he remounted, Sturgis looked carefully to his revolver; he even tried its balance, and after that unnecessary precaution, he climbed into the saddle again and sent the pinto down the trail once more, at the long, lazy lope which held on through the morning, rocking up hill and down dale until they came to the forking of the road. There was no problem here. As though to help his pursuers, the rider of the long-stepping horse had taken the curve short—his prints lay on the side of the road, far from all others, and the sheriff, without letting his pinto fall even into a trot, swung down the left-hand way toward the hills.

Two miles farther on, the sign disappeared on the road, and the sheriff cut in a small circle which brought him to a group of bushes and, in the middle of this, a spot of bare sand. There was not a single indentation on this sand, but the sheriff appeared to be greatly interested in it. He looked on all sides, and saw no other sign of shrubbery; then he dismounted, and searching among the brush he came upon a dry stalk broken across close to the surface of the ground.

The wood was so rotten that it was impossible to tell whether or not it had recently been broken, so the sheriff turned and looked fixedly at the center of the sand plot. It showed no sign; there was not the faintest indication of a mound, and sufficient wind had touched the surface to cover it with the tiny wind marks, in long, wavy lines. But apparently the sheriff had reduced his problem to a point where the clue must lie in the sand of this little opening. He stepped directly to the center, dug his toe into the ground, and turned up a quantity of charred sticks.

4

Sheriff Sturgis sent the pinto back to the road, and now the little horse broke from a lope into a gallop, still almost effortless, but nearly twice as rapid as his former gait. Once the sheriff glanced back; but the sun was comfortably high—it was not far past noon.

A full two hundred yards, or more, he had gone before he found the place where the pursued man had cut back onto the road again, and now the sheriff watched the tracks with a new interest. He found, as he had expected, that the gait was no longer a full gallop, but only a hand-canter, and Sturgis knew perfectly well that the long back and the fragile legs of such a horse could not stand the gait which was so natural to a cow pony.

The rider must have realized this, for presently the marks of the canter went out, and in its place was the sign of a trot. At this gait the animal went along much

better. There was an ample distance from print to
print, and the uniform size of the gap showed that he
had still plenty of strength left. Or perhaps his strength
was already far gone and the horse was traveling on
nerve alone.

However that might be, the sheriff soon ceased to
look at the tracks. Instead, he kept his eyes fastened far
down the road, and wherever it rolled out of sight
among the hills he sat straighter in the saddle and his
gaze became more piercing. There were many places
where a wary man could take shelter and watch a great
stretch of the road behind him; and if the fugitive were
anyone of this neighborhood, he would be sure to know
the sheriff by his celebrated pinto. In that case a wise
man would take no further chances, but pull his rifle
and wait for a shot.

So the sheriff, as he went deeper into the hills,
spurred the pinto to a faster gait; he looked back now
and again, to the road, and saw in two places a milling
of many tracks where the pursued had dismounted to
breathe his horse; and now he came swinging over the
shoulder of a hill, with a stretch of full three miles
running straight ahead of him. It was quite empty—not
a sign of any living thing in all its distance, but the
sheriff swung the pony around with a jerk and headed
back behind the hill.

He had planned to catch sight of the fugitive within
the next half hour of riding unless the sign he had read
had lied to him, and this gap of empty road startled
him. For it told him either that he had not read the
tracks correctly or that his quarry had left the road;
and if he had left the road there could only be two
reasons for it. One was that he had decided on a long
rest for himself and his mount, which was quite unrea-

sonable at this period of the day; the other was that he had seen the sheriff following, and had recognized the bright coloring of the pinto. The later reason was by far the best, and the sheriff acted upon it.

Leaving his pinto ensconced in a clump of trees on the far side of the hill, he skirted around the other edge. The road was a slightly graded cut on the side of a long, sharp slope, forested thickly, and the chances were great that the rider of the horse, if indeed he were a fugitive from justice, and if his mount were the chestnut of Jan van Zandt, would go either for rest or to spy on the pursuit among the trees above the road, where he could see everything and remain himself unseen.

It was on this side of the road, then, that Sturgis prepared to hunt, but he paused before beginning, partly because of the danger which lay ahead of him, and far more because, above all things in this world, he hated to go on foot.

It was while he stood among the brush at the roadside, summoning his resolution, and letting his bright little eyes rove everywhere among the trees, that the sheriff saw a man step out of the forest and go swinging down the road not fifty yards ahead of him. He was so set for the work in hand, however, that he had almost dismissed the stranger from his mind and started toward the trees when something in the gait of the man made him pause; it was a hobbling gait, short steps that were uneven, and the sheriff recognized through sympathy the pace of a man who generally moves only on horseback. More than this, he saw those strides gradually lengthen, as the walker swung into his work, and it convinced the sharp eyes of the sheriff that this was no random hunter, strolling over the mountains, but a man who had recently climbed from the back of a horse, and whose leg muscles were not yet all straightened out.

Not until he had noted all these facts, did the sheriff catch the gleam of spurs, but he had already made up his mind. When he left his horse, he had taken his rifle with him; now he deliberately dropped upon one knee behind a shrub and sighted among the branches.

With the stock squeezed into his shoulder and his finger curling on the trigger he shouted: "Halt!"

It brought an amazing result. Instead of turning with both hands held high over his head, as is the time-honored custom on such occasions, the stranger leaped to one side, at the same time pitching toward the ground and whirling about on his face; so that he struck with only his left elbow supporting his shoulders, and in that hair's breadth of time, he had conjured a forty-five Colt out of its holster. He lay with the muzzle of the revolver tipped up and down, balancing for a snap shot in any direction.

"Not so bad," called the sheriff.

The man with the revolver twisted to one side, and the revolver became rigid; for the echo from the hillside had made Sturgis' voice seem to come from the opposite direction.

"Drop it," continued the sheriff. "I've got a line on you, Bud. I've got your head in the circle, pal."

The other hesitated for a single instant, and then scrambled to his feet, tossing the revolver into the dust.

"Well," he said coolly enough, "what does all this mean?"

"It means that I want the other gun," said the sheriff.

"What gun?"

"Don't play me for a fool," Sturgis retorted. "First, turn your face the other way."

He was obeyed.

"Now, shell out your other cannon."

The man produced a second weapon from somewhere in his clothes, and tossed it away.

"All right," said the sheriff, stepping from behind the bush, "you can face this way, friend, after you've got those hands up high."

The hands went up slowly, and with equal slowness the other turned. Sturgis, with intense interest, saw that the fellow had to fight, apparently, before he could force his hands above the level of his shoulders and up into the region of helplessness.

"If you want my money," said the stranger without undue nervousness, "you'll find my wallet in the left hip pocket."

"Thanks," said Sturgis. "Don't mind if I do. Get up them hands!"

The arms of the other had, in fact, lowered a little as the sheriff came closer; but now he straightened them again and looked thoughtfully at Sturgis. He was in all respects a man of superior appearance, with a carefully tended mustache, kept clean of the lips, and a pale, rather handsome face with those square cheeks, somewhat puffy at the jowls, which betoken good living. Above all, he had that straight and penetrating glance which comes to men who have directed many others. He kept his hands high up while the fingers of the sheriff ran swiftly over him; he did not even quiver when Sturgis extracted a third weapon—it was a little, double-barreled pistol which hung under the man's shirt suspended from a noose of horsehair.

Sturgis knew now why the man was so averse to

getting his hands above his shoulders, for even if his thumb was as high as his throat he had still a chance to hook it under the little horsehair lariat and whip out the pistol for the two final shots.

"My, my," sighed the sheriff, as he cut the string and pocketed the little weapon. "Kind of a walkin' arsenal, ain't you?"

"In this country, apparently," the other replied, "a man needs to be."

"Oh, we ain't so bad around here," said the sheriff. "For instance, we don't lift hosses regular."

There was not a flicker of the other's eyes.

"Suppose you lead me where the chestnut is," Sturgis said. "All right now. You can take your hands down."

"Thanks," said the man of the well-trimmed mustache, and he brushed it with his fingertips, studying the sheriff. "For a hold-up man," he said, "you talk in a singular fashion. What chestnut do you refer to?"

The smile of the sheriff widened to a broad grin. "I'm forty-five years old, partner," he said. "If I was two years younger I think you'd get by, but today you're out of luck. The seat of your trousers is all shiny, the way cloth gets when it rubs on leather, say; and they's a sort of hoss smell about you. I say, lead me to that hoss and don't be aggravatin'."

The other shrugged his shoulders and gave up.

"It's not worth seeing," he said.

"Dead?"

"It was a show horse," said the stranger. His jaw thrust out and his face changed. "The first time in my life that I've gone so wrong in judging a horse."

"No stamina, eh?" murmured the sheriff sympathetically. "No guts at all; well, I ain't surprised that you went wrong on him. When them hosses first come into the country they took my eye, too; then I seen what a day's work does to 'em and I changed my mind. But I didn't hear no shot; how'd you kill the hoss?"

"I couldn't risk a bullet," said the other. "Sound travels too far in this country."

"And instead?"

"A knife turned the trick nicely—through the temple, you know."

The sheriff opened both his mouth and his eyes. "You run a knife into that hossflesh?" he muttered, recovering himself. "Well, it's time we started back; sorry you got to walk."

"Not at all," replied the other, apparently unmoved by the hardening of the sheriff's voice. "I'm not going to walk, and I'm not going back."

5

The nonchalant speech made the sheriff look again at his prisoner. "Tut, tut," he said good-naturedly, "you s'prise me, partner. What d'you figure on doin'?"

"Sitting down on that rock and talking to you."

"It'll get us back to the town after dark," said the sheriff, "but outside of that, it's a hog-ear to me whether you walk back now or after we've talked."

They made themselves comfortable on the rock, each twisting round so that his face was to the other.

"Now, what d'you want to do?" said the sheriff.

"I want your horse."

"Yes?"

"And I want you to take back to Sloan the price of the horse I've just ridden to death, along with the price of your own horse."

"Oh," murmured the sheriff mildly, "maybe you'll give me a check?"

The stranger did not smile. "Here's my wallet," he said.

"You count it for me," suggested Sturgis.

So the thief unfolded the leather, and extracting a thick wad of greenbacks, he counted over silently and slowly into the sheriff's hand five bills of one thousand dollars each and thirty more of the hundred-dollar denomination.

"One thousand dollars for the dead horse," said the stranger, "one hundred for your horse, and six thousand, nine hundred dollars to pay for your long walk back to Sloan." He raised his eyes from the count, retaining a few bills in his hand.

The sheriff laid the money back on his knee with a sigh. "Sorry," he said.

"Naturally you're sorry that I should underestimate your dislike for walking," said the stranger calmly. "Accordingly, I hasten to correct the mistake," and he added to the little pack four more bills of a thousand dollars each. "Ten thousand, nine hundred is the price of that walk back to Sloan. And now, if you'll pardon me, I'll take your horse and hurry along."

The sheriff sat with his shoulders bowed; he looked like a man over whom old age had suddenly swept, unstringing all his nerves, and he squinted up at the stranger with eyes of pain. "Sit down again," said the sheriff huskily. "I hate to say it, but you've no idea how I hate walkin'."

The other sighed; then he sat down and leaned a little closer. "I want you to take note of these things," he said, and checked them off on the tips of his fingers. "Did you ever hear of a horse thief with close to eleven thousand dollars in his wallet? Does it seem possible to you that a man might be making a journey in such desperate haste that he would change saddles from one horse to another without stopping to haggle with the owner of the second horse about a price? Finally, do you think it absurd and beyond reason that a man making such a desperate journey would, when it is completed, send back the price of the horse he had taken?"

"I'll tell you what," said the sheriff, "them are three questions that twelve men could answer better than one."

For the first time the stranger flushed. He sat back, gritting his teeth, and looked the sheriff straight in the eyes. "I have a checkbook with me," he said at length. "Name the price of that walk back to Sloan. It'll be yours."

"H-m-m," murmured the sheriff, "I'd a sort of an idea that it would come down to a matter of writing a check."

"Because," said the other earnestly, "you know that my check for almost any amount would be good." He clenched one hand into a fist while he talked, and the sheriff, looking down, wondered at the smallness of the hand, and the whiteness of the skin. "Besides," went on the stranger, "in your heart you're absolutely convinced that what I've told you is the truth; you know that I'm here on business only; you know from my appearance that I'm not a horse rustler; you know that I'm talking to you as straight as my money talks."

"Straighter, in fact," said the sheriff.

The stranger flushed again. "If you're offended because I've attempted to bribe you," he said, "I'm sorry. But I've most urgent need to get across those hills; I couldn't stop to be scrupulous."

"D'you ever notice," said the sheriff absently, "that when a gent starts elbowin' in a crowd most generally he starts a fight that everybody gets hurt in?"

The stranger caught his breath with impatience but said nothing.

"It's that way about the chestnut hoss," went on the sheriff. "He ain't worth more'n a thousand dollars, that hoss that you turned into so much meat—with your knife! No, he ain't hardly worth more'n a thousand, but maybe he means more'n money to the gent that raised him from the time he was a foal. You see?"

The stranger nodded, yet it was evident that he did not altogether get the sheriff's viewpoint.

"Look at it another way," Sturgis continued. "You grab this hoss and ride on, expectin' to pay for him later. Well, the gent that owns this hoss finds him gone and right off he says that a gent near by is the one that done the stealin'. He's sure of that, because he knows this young gent hates him. Well, he starts out and rounds up a pile of ornery boys like himself and they come boilin' down to my office bent on revenge. They go one way; I go the other. I have all the luck, it turns out. Now, suppose that gang of farmers misses the hoss—which they will—and comes back thinkin' a lot of hard things about the young gent that they first thought done the stealin'? Well, people take it kind of hard around here when a hoss is stolen, and when they got a suspicion they don't always wait for a jury; they go straight to Judge Lynch and get an opinion. You foller me, maybe?"

"I do," said the other, frowning. "You think there'll be a lynching party on account of this chestnut horse?"

His face convulsed as he spoke, and for a moment the sheriff sat with his mouth parted over his next word, staring at the stranger. He seemed to see new things in the horse thief; as if it were the middle of night and a match had been lighted under that face.

"I got to tell you another side of it," said the sheriff. "Suppose the bunch of farmers don't lynch this gent I'm talking about, but they only muss him up a lot and call him names. Well, he's the kind of a boy that takes hard names to heart terrible bad."

"If I'm not mistaken," said the stranger, "this young fellow won't use his gun more than once in your district. You're the sheriff, I take it."

"My name is Sturgis," the sheriff replied. There was no change in the horse thief's expression. "Yes, I'm the sheriff and my record is pretty long and pretty clean."

"I'm sure it is," the stranger agreed earnestly.

"But," went on Sturgis, "if all the gents I've ever taken was rolled into one, all their tricks, and all their speed with guns, and all their coolheadedness, and all their cussedness—if they was all rolled into one I'd rather tackle them all over again than tackle this same young gent."

The stranger rubbed his chin nervously with his knuckles and then replied: "I begin to understand what you mean—but I'd like to see this remarkable young man.

"Oh, he ain't so different," said the sheriff. "He ain't so different from the rest; he's just a split-second faster with his gun; he's just an inch closer to the bell with his slug; he's just a quiver steadier in his hand; he's just a dash cooler in the head." He sighed. "It's surprisin' what a lot of difference a few little things make when

they're all added up. You see, this boy had a considerable pile of an inheritance, and he improves a lot on
what he got for a start."

"That description reminds me of someone I knew,"
the stranger said musingly.

"Was it, maybe, La Paloma that you knew?" murmured
the sheriff innocently.

The eyes of the other scanned the face of the sheriff
with a swift, peculiar glance. "No," he said, "who was
La Paloma?"

"I'll tell you what," said the sheriff suddenly, "in spite
of all the harm that maybe you've done by stealin' that
hoss, I can't help lettin' my heart go out to a gent that
knows how rotten it is to walk on foot."

"Ah?" murmured the other. Then he drew out a
folded checkbook.

"Suppose," said the sheriff, "that I had some dice
here, I might take a chance to see whether you take
my hoss or whether you come back to Sloan with
me."

"We could flip a coin," said the stranger.

"Too risky," murmured the sheriff. "If we even had a
pack of cards we could get along."

"Ah," murmured the stranger, and instantly a black
leather case of playing cards was in the palm of his
hand.

"So," sighed the sheriff. "Kind of looks like you've
took me up. What'll we play to decide?"

"Something short?" suggested the other.

"Sure."

"Anything you say will do with me," said the horse
thief. "But wait a moment—why not cut for the first
ace?"

He broke off with a frown, for he suddenly discovered

that the sheriff was smiling quietly, straight into his eyes.

"D'you know," said the sheriff, "that I been waiting for this minute for years and years?"

"What?"

"You was always a queer one," murmured Sturgis, "but still I can't understand why you'd ever come back here, Pat."

6

The silence which followed had an acid quality; it seemed to eat into the mind of the stranger and weaken him; presently he moistened his white lips, and whispered a curse.

"Don't do it," said the sheriff, shaking his head. "Don't talk like that, because it always makes me sort of uneasy when a gent cusses me—even an old acquaintance like you, Pat."

Then he added, after a moment, during which he looked almost longingly at the other: "Well, I guess we'd better be goin' back. D'you remember that it was in a place about like this that we—"

"Wait!" Pat gasped and reached his hand out toward the sheriff, but before it touched, his fingers relaxed, and the arm remained suspended in midair. "It can't end like this!" he cried. "It can't end like this!" His whole body was shaking, but all at once he straight-

ened, and his mustache stopped working and bristling.
"You're waiting for me to break down, are you?"

The sheriff raised a deprecating hand. "A man like
you break down? A scholar and a gentleman like you?
Sure I ain't waitin' to see that. I'd be a fool, wouldn't I?"

"Ed, it all happened twenty years ago. It's dead."

"She's dead," agreed the sheriff, nodding.

The other groaned and clenched his fists.

"It takes about twenty years for a good wine to get
ripe and all softened down so's a man can enjoy it," said
the sheriff calmly.

The horse thief appeared to be buried in thought.
"Suppose I were to tell you a story of a fellow who was
down and out—who'd done some rotten things while
he was young—who straightened up and tried to be a
man afterward—"

"Go on," broke in the sheriff. "You was always a fine
talker, Pat," he added encouragingly. "You'd ought to
make a good yarn out of it. Let's hear it, Langley."

"You know me too well to think I'd whine," said Pat
Langley.

"Sure I do."

"I want you to see in one glance what you do if you
take me into Sloan and drag up that other matter
against me. Out in the West Indies on the island of St.
Hilaire I have one of the finest plantations in the whole
place; I have a wife and daughter." He drew a second
little leather case from an inside pocket. "You'll see
their pictures on one side of the card and the picture of
my house on the other." He handed the case to the
sheriff. "I want you to know that you'll be stepping into
the happiest home in St. Hilaire and ruining two lives,
beside mine. But if you'll drop this affair, Ed, you'll
step through the doors you see in that picture and

halve everything that's inside. If you don't want to be near me—and I don't suppose you will—you get half of my bank account. More than that. You can see my financial statement and make your own terms. I'm not offering this as a bribe. In the first place, I did you a great wrong; I want to make amends for that wrong, and the only way I can do it is to work on the financial end. At the same time, I want you to see that after I wronged you I realized what I had done. I did go straight."

But the sheriff gave back the unopened leather case.

"I couldn't look into a woman's face just now, Pat," he said gently.

Langley paled as though he had gained a first glimpse into the mind of the other. A change came gradually over his face. The sheriff, watching in fascination, noted that change and dropped his hand for the first time upon his rifle stock; but always he had kept the muzzle directed at the horse thief.

Yet Langley only said: "Throw me the makings, will you? See if I've forgotten how to roll 'em."

The sheriff obeyed without a word and watched him deftly make his smoke and light it. When he had inhaled the first breath Langley seemed to find a new cheer. He raised his head and looked about him as he exhaled the blue-brown vapor slowly.

"Not so bad," he said. "Better than a lot of the tailor-mades I smoke." He met the eye of the sheriff. "And now that I'm back in it," he said, "this same country isn't so bad. Cleaner air around here than we have in the islands." He drew a long breath and puffed it out again. "Well, when did you spot me first, Ed? I knew you the moment I saw you, but I depended on the twenty years and this mustache—like a fool! I knew you when I was putting my hands up and I hesitated about making a try with that little necklace of mine. Well, when did you know me first?"

"You're a hard man, ain't you, Pat?" said the sheriff quietly. "When it comes to the pinch, wife and child can go hang."

"You thought I'd weaken, didn't you?" He chuckled.

"It wasn't your face that told on you," said the sheriff, "though it gave me a bit of a shock. Made me start thinking. First of all, when you threw yourself on the ground. That made me guess—that old trick, you know. But all those things were hints pilin' up in the back of my head. Then I got my first real clue when you twisted your eyes at me when I mentioned La Paloma. Funny way you have of glintin' at a gent out of the corner of your eyes, Pat. But what sewed the thing up in my mind was the cards. You always used to have cards with you, and if it came to a choice in a pinch you liked to cut for aces."

The horse thief looked calmly at him and tossed his cigarette butt away.

"Speaking of cards," he said, "I wonder if she knew that you'd played cards that night?"

The rifle trembled in the hands of the sheriff, but Langley did not wince.

"I was drunk," the sheriff replied.

The other chuckled. "We've all heard that sort of talk."

Sturgis began to breathe through his mouth, as though he had been running.

"To go back to the beginning," said the horse thief, "suppose you and I were to have an even break for our guns. Just you and me with nobody to look on. We take anything for a signal to start for the butts—say the next time that hawk screams. And the fellow who drops is left for the buzzards. If you get me—why, you did it making an arrest of a horse thief; if I get you, I take pinto along over the hills."

"I'd like the idea," Sturgis sighed. "Heaven knows how I been prayin' for it twenty years!"

"Good old sport!" Langley said as he rose. "It's done, then?"

"Wait a minute. In the old days you was always a bit better with a gun than me, Pat."

"But you've had more practice lately."

"You lie," said the sheriff, without heat. "You practice with a gun every day of your life. You have to."

The other flushed, looked swiftly about him, and then saw that he was helpless.

"But aside from that," went on the sheriff, "I think the way of the law is a pretty good way, mostly. It gets at the inside of some gents in a way that powder and lead can't. Suppose I was to blow your head off. You wouldn't feel nothin'. I'd feel sort of better afterward, but what would you feel? Nothin'! But s'pose you get sent up for a little while—for stealin' a hoss. That wouldn't be bad. Not the prison, but after you got out, St. Hilaire would have the news. I'd take care that they did. You're proud, ain't you, Pat?"

"I'd kill you," said the other thoughtfully. "I'd kill you as sure as heaven when I was out."

"I don't cross no bridges till I come to 'em," the sheriff replied. "Besides, I know the warden of the state prison. Maybe he'd let me come up and pay you friendly visits once in a while. And then maybe I'd get so fond of havin' you where I could see you that I'd hate to see you leave. So I might want to dig back twenty years and get something else that would hold you the rest of your life. Or if I got tired of seein' you that way, I might even get something that would hang you, Pat." He bit off a large corner of his Virginia leaf and stowed it gingerly in his cheek. "You see how many sides they is to the thing, Pat?" he said gently.

"I see one thing," said the other, with equal calm. "Twenty years has drilled through your thick head and put some sense there."

"Well, the day's wearin' on. S'pose we start back. I hate to make you walk."

"Don't mind me," said Pat heartily. "I generally walk every day on the island, and I'm in pretty fair trim."

The sheriff climbed on his horse, and as he did so, the other stepped to the side of the road, whistling, and leaned over.

"Stand up!" called the sheriff.

The other slowly stood up and showed his teeth under the black mustache. He kicked the revolver away. "I almost had it," he confided to the sheriff.

"My, my!" murmured Sturgis, smiling. "Wasn't that a close chance, now? I'll tell a man!"

He motioned down the road ahead of him.

"Certainly," said the horse thief, "I always like to go first." And he stepped out into the road.

"The same old Pat," the sheriff said reminiscently. "You was always prime company."

7

The things which the sheriff did not know about the farming element around the town of Sloan were supplied to him by a seventh sense. It all fell out as he had warned the horse thief.

First the posse, led by red-bearded Rex Houlahan, swept like a storm down the valley. They rode hard and they rode well, and they had the fastest horses within two hundred miles of Sloan, except Prince Harry himself. In fact, the six were chosen men of courage, for, in recruiting his posse, Jan van Zandt had not even applied to the cattlemen, knowing their answer beforehand, and of the farmers, these six were the only ones who cared to come within rifle range of Jeremiah Peyton.

Jan van Zandt knew how to pick his men both for the horses they rode and for their personal grit; and one day he might sit in the state legislature for just such qualities as he showed in this crisis.

He wanted Prince Harry back. The horse was the culmination of a long labor of breeding that ran back through two generations of the van Zandt family, and it would take another two generations to get him back; but the affair was more than the matter of one horse. It was the culmination of the ill feeling between the two main classes of population around the little town.

To be sure, the majority on both sides remained quiescent. Of the farmers there were only the six; and of the cattlemen there was only Jeremiah Peyton; but if matters came to a showdown the entire populace was apt to rise in arms and a class war result. The imagination of the sheriff had not stretched as far as this, but the calculation of Jan van Zandt had, and he figured that in the ultimate struggle the odds would be with the farmers in about the same proportion—six to one. However, as far as the sheriff's predictions ran, they were correct.

The posse rushed down the valley, flogging their spirited nags every jump of the way. When they reached the end of the valley, where the foothills sprawled out to a flat and the muddy old Winton River went straggling into the desert beyond, they drew rein and looked about them. There was still no sign of a chestnut horse before them; and when Rex Houlahan looked down to the road he did not find a trace of a recent hoofprint before them.

There was a rumble in the posse, but few words, and they turned back up the valley. At the town of Winton they stopped for lunch—it was already afternoon—and lay about, mumbling threats against the universe in general and thieving cattlemen in particular.

In the afternoon they started on up the valley. No sooner had they taken the road than they discovered new grievances all brought upon them by the scoundrel who had stolen the chestnut stallion. Their horses were stiff and sore from the unusual hard work of the morning; their delicate limbs were meant for it no more than the legs of Prince Harry had been meant to stall off the dogged pursuit of the sheriff's pinto.

Rex Houlahan's bay mare had been raised from a delicate foal like a child in the family; now she was desperately lame in the off foreleg and Rex went stamping down the road on foot, gnashing his teeth behind his red beard, with the mare following him like a dog. Within a mile she was going chiefly upon three legs, her head nodding far down at each step, and Houlahan's heart was too full for utterance.

For some reason, none of the other five cared to break in before the big Irishman. They let him walk ahead, and they followed in a somber group. For five miles not a word was said, and then, without sound or signal, the whole procession stopped in the road; the bay mare lay down at once in the dust. As for Houlahan, he turned and cast one long look at his horse; then he noted that they were opposite the house of Jeremiah Peyton.

In fact, any one with half an eye could see the master of the shack sitting on the front veranda, tilted back as usual against the wall. To be sure the chestnut stallion was not in sight, but, as the posse had explained to the sheriff that morning, the absence of the horse proved nothing. He might have been passed on to confederates in the foothills beyond, thieving cowpunchers who well knew how to send horses along by subterranean courses and bring them out a hundred miles or more away to be sold innocently to the first high bidder.

All these things ate into the hearts of the farmers as they sat the saddle, breathing the pungent alkali dust which the feet of their weary horses stirred up; and most of all the idle form of Jeremiah stirred them. Idleness in their Middle Western scheme of things was the all-surpassing sin. Then Rex Houlahan cursed once, softly, and started across the fields. The others followed him.

How it happened that Jeremiah Peyton, the son of Hank Peyton, himself the chief figure of many a tale of border war against the Mexicans, calmly sat on his porch without a weapon near, while he watched six of his enemies come across his land toward him, no one in Sloan could ever imagine. Men were to scratch their heads over this mystery for days and days. The only explanation lay in the profound contempt which he felt for these "dirt grubbers" and "land hogs," as he had been known to call them to their faces. He did not even look up until they were close to the porch; and when he did look up he did not rise; he merely whittled on at his stick.

First he looked at the tops of their hats, then he whistled to the sky, then he called negligently to an old yellow cur which skulked across the porch away from the strangers; last of all he appeared to notice the silent stationary group sitting in their saddles, armed to the teeth, before his porch. Most of all, there was Rex Houlahan on foot, and nearest to him. Although the loss was Jan van Zandt's, Houlahan was the spokesman.

"Peyton," he said.

The boy looked into the face of the big man and

smiled, but did not answer. It was a needless insult, and the hands of the posse gathered their weapons closer.

"Peyton, we've come for you," Houlahan said.

For the first time the meaning of the men came to Jeremiah Peyton. In truth, he had despised them all so heartily that up to this point he refused to let his reason tell him what the general silence and the guns meant. Even now, as he stood up and stretched the muscles of his magnificent, lithe body from fingertips to toes, he felt that he could dispose of them all, his naked hands against their guns; but the puniest man in the world, if he is possessed of a rage which does not pour itself forth in words, will command the respect of the strongest man. Peyton looked again, grudgingly admitted that the six were picked men of their kind, and that they were dangerous.

"Evening," he said, running his eyes calmly from face to face. "Climb off your horses and rest yourselves."

"We'll rest when we're through with you," Houlahan replied.

Up to that time he himself did not exactly know why he had led the way to confront Peyton, but as soon as he spoke, the words struck fire in him. The growl of the posse behind him urged him on, and in another moment mob frenzy had them all by the throats.

"Particularly me," interjected Jan van Zandt.

Perhaps if Jeremiah had returned the soft answer, he might have turned away wrath; instead of that he saw the spark of fire in every eye and deliberately chose to pour oil upon the flame.

"Before you're through with me," he said, smiling in his odd manner straight at the brown-faced farmer, "you'll be an old man—or buzzard food. Get away from that door!"

For Houlahan had slipped over until he was near the front door of the house, thus hemming the master of the place against the wall. As Jeremiah spoke he swept his hand behind him, to the hip, and seemed to close his fingers over something.

"The rest of you," he ordered, "get off my land before I drill you for disturbin' my peace!" And, in the midst of the crisis and his bluff, he grinned at his own joke.

They had scattered back like fire before wind. Every man was behind his horse or getting there as fast as he could, and Houlahan, with a moan of anxiety, reached one of the small wooden pillars which supported the roof of the veranda, and seemed to be hiding there—hiding from the slug of a Colt forty-five behind four inches of rotten pine!

Even now Jeremiah would have been safe if he had used this moment of confusion to leap to the door and into the house. That would have begun a battle of which the mountain desert would still be talking; but with his heart swelling with scorn he stood there and laughed in their faces and waved them away.

Then Houlahan saw from the side that there was no bulge of a gun on Peyton's hip and he screamed in a voice gone thin and piping with exultation. "He's bluffin' without a gun! Take him alive!"

The posse waited for no second invitation. The alarm of the instant before had strung their nerves to the breaking point, and now that the fear of bullets was removed, they flung themselves from their horses and plunged at Jerry. He would have stayed there to meet them even at these odds, but he had that Western horror of being overmatched by physical force, of being reduced to impotence by numbers. He sprang like a tiger for the door and Houlahan rushed to meet him with a wailing cry, like one who struggles in a lost cause.

There was a base of bulldog in Houlahan; a driving blow met him as he came in, and the whipping knuckles of Jerry laid the cheekbone bare, but though Houlahan fell, he fell forward and clutched blindly with both arms. The arms wound around the legs of Jerry, and though he dropped Houlahan the rest of the way to the floor with a crushing blow behind the ear, the Irishman had done his work.

Before Jerry could shake his feet clear and gain the door, the five were on him. He swung about as the avalanche struck. He broke the nose of Pete Goodwin; he slashed wildly at Pierre la Roche and Gus Saunders; he sent Eric Jensen rolling away with his arms clasped about his midriff; and then Jan van Zandt came up behind Jerry, raised his forty-five like a club, and Jerry went down, inert.

After that, Jan stood guard, with the muzzle of his weapon pointed at the head of the cowman, while the rest of them picked up Houlahan.

Even after Jerry himself had recovered enough to sit up and sneer at the revolver which Jan van Zandt pointed at his head, Houlahan was still the object of main interest. At length they patched up the gashed side of his face, though blood still trickled beneath the bandage which they had made from one of Jerry's sheets. But even after he had gained his feet, Houlahan came staggering, punch-drunk, and wavered before Jerry, the son of Hank.

"Ah, man, ah, man!" Rex Houlahan said. "That was a wallop ye handed me!" He grinned a lopsided grin at Jerry, and then seemed to realize for the first time where he was and what had happened. "Tarnation!" he gasped. "I thought I was back in Brooklyn at old Rinkenstein's saloon. Now, you, get up on your hind legs." And he stirred the captive with the toe of his boot.

"The spur's the thing for that," put in Jan van Zandt, and though Jerry was already rising, he assisted by rolling the rowel of his spur across Jerry's leg. Little pinpoints of crimson began to show through the cloth, and the posse laughed.

8

A moment later they were silent, stunned, as they realized that Jerry had risen to his feet in perfect silence. Neither the touch with the toe of the boot nor the spur nor the burst of laughter had brought a word from him.

One by one they began to realize that, unless they killed this man, he would most infallibly kill them.

"Get a rope," Jan van Zandt ordered. It was not the first time in his life nor was it the last that he would seize the highest note of public opinion and give it a voice.

A rope was found and a tree likewise, and they brought Jerry beneath a promising branch. Of the six men, five, at least, were anxious to get the thing done with as quickly as possible, but somewhere in the depth of Houlahan a spark of revolt rose.

"Is this a lynchin', maybe?" he asked, as Jan van

Zandt placed the noose over the neck of Jerry Peyton. "It ain't," he answered himself. "This is justice. It being justice, he's got a right to be heard. Ain't that the law for hoss thieves?"

"They ain't any law for hoss thieves," remarked Gus Saunders. "But make him talk, if you want to. It'll be amusin' to hear him lie."

"Sure," Houlahan said. "All right, lad. Come out with the truth! Did you steal Prince Harry?"

The accused smiled in the face of the Irishman.

"Speak up," said Houlahan. "If you can prove that you didn't—which you can't—we'll let you go free." He stepped back, astonished. "Are you goin' to let yourself swing without sayin' a word?" he asked. "Are you goin' to give up a chance to talk for your life?"

The glance of Jerry Peyton went from face to face in the group and the farmers stirred uneasily. They knew that he was examining their features so closely that neither time nor beard could ever mask them from him. If his destruction had been a matter of mob pleasure before, it now became a cold duty. They looked at one another, and they found the same answer in every eye.

"But he's got to speak up," protested Houlahan. He touched his bandaged cheek tenderly and then went on. "If he don't want to confess, make him. Listen to me, partner, talk out and you'll have the weight of the crime off your soul. You'll die so easy you won't feel the rope hardly."

The same faint, derisive smile met him.

"Let me try him," Jan van Zandt offered. "The things he don't answer we'll figure is answered 'yes.' You all take note of that because the sheriff may want to ask us some questions later on. Here, you!"

The eyes of the prisoner were focused far above the head of the big farmer, and now van Zandt caught Jerry by the chin and twisted his head. "Look me the eye and tell whatever truth there is in your lying heart. You hate me, don't you?"

Not a muscle of Jerry's face altered.

"You see?" said Jan van Zandt. "He admits that he hates me—Jan van Zandt, a peaceful, law-abidin' citizen! That'll be remembered. Next, did a horse of yours get killed by accident on my place?"

Jerry maintained his contemptuous silence.

Van Zandt turned to the others. "He admits that a horse of his was killed on my place. Keep all this in mind because it's leadin' somewhere. Now listen to me, Peyton: Did you refuse to go to court like an honest man and get your price for the horse that was killed?"

His triumph shone in his bronze face as he nodded to the posse, after pausing for the answer that did not come. "You hear that? Now listen! Did you write to me afterward that you would get your own price for the mare? You did. They's other witnesses to that. Last of all: Did you wait till you got the chance and then steal Prince Harry, that's worth ten times anything your mongrel buckskin was ever worth?"

The smile of infinite contempt played again over the lips of Jeremiah. Jan van Zandt, with a sob of grief and hate, drew back his heavy arm and struck the prisoner across the mouth. It threw the body of Jerry back against the rope, but when he staggered erect again, though a white mark enclosed his mouth, there was still the ghost of the smile upon it. It was not the patience of the martyr; it was that sort of stifled rage which overwhelms a man and makes him cold. He found an unexpected intercessor here, for

Rex Houlahan caught the arm of the big farmer and jerked him back.

"Don't do that again," he said savagely. "He's got his hands tied behind him, ain't he? He's helpless. He's going to be hung like the hoss thief that he is, but I ain't goin' to stand by and see him insulted—not a man with a wallop like the one he packs." He grinned at Jerry with something akin to affection. "Nobody can hit like that unless it's born in him, Jerry. It's a shame you can't live to fight in the ring. But there's one thing more, boys. We can't string him up until he's confessed. It ain't right, and I won't stand for it. He's got to say enough to save his soul—if it can be saved. Besides, we'll need more than dumb talk when the sheriff asks his questions."

"Make him talk, then," said Jan van Zandt, "but don't lay hands on me again. It ain't healthy, not by a long ways."

"I've laid hands on worse ones than you, son," said the Irishman as he bent his attention on the prisoner. "Lad, I give you the last chance. Will you talk, or do we have to make you talk?"

And when Jerry remained silent, Houlahan gave directions swiftly and the others obeyed. They fixed running nooses in both ends of another rope, threw it over the branch, and tightened the nooses around the wrists of Jerry. One jerk brought him off the ground, his long body, with the arms above his head, swaying back and forth; he seemed gigantic. There were two men on one rope and three on the other. Houlahan stood in front of the prisoner and talked up to him; he had control, being the inventor of the expedient.

"Jerry," he said, "I see you're fighting hard. You'll

stave it off for a while because your arms are strong. But pretty soon the muscles begin to crack, they get that tired, and then they give way and the pull comes under your armpits. Then you feel it down your ribs and across your shoulder blades. Then it takes you in the joints of the shoulders and you begin to think your arms are comin' out of the sockets. You're a heavy man, Jerry, and when your muscles give out, and your hands feel dead, you'll have all that weight just hangin' on the tendons around the shoulder. Boy, don't be a fool. Talk up. Say what you done. Tell me the truth. Whisper it, if you don't want the rest of 'em to hear, and I'll never tell a soul. But you got to tell the truth before you die; you got to, or we'll keep you up there by the wrists until you yell for the pain of it!"

As he approached the latter end of his talk he grew more violent, raising his voice; but when he ceased, there was still no response from Jerry. After that Houlahan stood under the motionless form and watched with his own face twisted into an agony of sympathy.

After a while, the shoulders of Jerry slumped down, and all his weight rested with a jerk on the joints. His muscles had given away at last, and though it brought a groan from Houlahan, there was not a sound from Jerry. Houlahan began to whisper advice—telling Jerry how impossible it was to resist—begging him to give up and speak. Then the head of Jerry, which had hitherto remained proudly erect, toppled forward with another jerk and remained hanging low. From behind, he looked like a headless form. Houlahan threw his arm across his face. He went toward the men at the ropes.

"Jan," he begged. "Go take my place. I can't stand it." And big Jan van Zandt went and stood under the body they were torturing. At the first upward glance he blinked and shrank back a step; but he came close again and looked steadily into the face of Jerry. He was so fascinated by what he saw that his own expression escaped his attention.

For some time the men at the ropes watched his change of face, and then, incredulously, they saw a smile come on the lips of Jan van Zandt. Houlahan cried out; with one accord the others slacked away and the limp form crumbled against the earth, the legs and arms falling into crazy positions, as though they were broken. Jerry had fainted. The Irishman straightened the limbs, and one by one the rest of the posse looked in his face and shuddered.

"They ain't a thing to do but wind him up this way," said Jan van Zandt, drawing his revolver. "He'll feel no more pain and we'll have done our duty. Stand away, boys, and turn your backs."

There was a whine from Houlahan as he came between van Zandt and his victim. The Irishman was sobbing with rage.

"So help me," he said, "but I think you like doin' this dirty work."

"I got a duty as a citizen to perform," Jan van Zandt said.

"You got a duty to be a man."

"D'you mean to say you want this—to live?"

"Let the law handle him. Turn him over to the law."

"They'll get no evidence. He'll be turned loose. D'you want the son of Hank Peyton on your trail, Rex?"

"If they don't keep him in jail," said Houlahan firmly, "he won't be able to use a gun for two weeks with them hands, and we'll have a chance to think of what's next. Heaven knows I don't want Peyton on my trail, but I'd rather you burned me by inches than have that face hauntin' me the rest of my life. Boys, get out the buckboard, and we'll take Peyton in to the sheriff."

They had spent their first fury in the rush on Jerry; and for the blows he gave them they had tortured him to senselessness. Pierre la Roche and Gus Saunders hitched two of Peyton's own mules to the buckboard they found behind the house; they placed him in the body of the wagon. La Roche drove, and Houlahan sat in the wagon watching the inert captive. The others followed with the horse slowly, and before they reached the town of Sloan, Eric Jensen and Pete Goodwin had dropped back and tried to fade away in the darkness. But the rest cursed them back into the procession. No one would be allowed to dodge his share of the responsibility.

"Suppose he dies," Houlahan had shouted from the wagon, "d'you think I'm goin' to be the only one to take his body in?"

So they closed up after that, and taking that mysterious comfort which comes out of numbers in any crisis, they began to talk about other things.

Finally the wagon reached the main street of Sloan. It was unavoidable. Before they had gone a hundred feet the word spread. Men, women, and children poured into the street. The word was taken up. The posse had caught the horse thief, and the horse thief was Jerry Peyton.

Men rode their horses beside the wagon and looked at the prostrate body within; then they stared at the faces of the posse and raised a cheer. Five minutes before the six farmers were beginning to drop toward despondency. Five minutes later they were trav-

eling in the midst of an ovation. Voices in the crowd
of townsfolk took up a shout for a lynching. They
wanted it then, and in the main street of the village.
But Rex Houlahan stood in the wagon with his red
beard blowing across his throat and no one made an
attempt to seize the thief. The wagon halted before
the jail.

9

Usually mob scenes did not attract the sheriff. It was a silent tribute to the remarkable noise which the crowd set up this day before the jail, that Ed Sturgis himself came through the heavy door and stood at the top of the wooden steps. His hat was pushed far back on his head, allowing his unruly hair to pour beneath the brim and straggle almost to his eyes.

It was always a sign of weariness when Ed Sturgis wore his hat in this way, and when he was weary he was not a pleasant man. The crowd was afflicted with the usual mob blindness, however; all it saw was the sheriff standing at the head of the steps with his hands on his hips, grinning down at them; and the mob gathered itself up in a big wave that washed up the steps and deposited six heroes all about Sturgis.

"They done it!" cried scores of voices. "They put one

over on you, Ed. They got the thief; they got Jerry Peyton!"

An unusual phenomenon followed. The wave of noise was met now by a contrary wave of silence which began in the immediate neighborhood of the sheriff and spreading first to those about him, gradually worked its way over the hundreds in the street. A path opened before Sturgis down the steps and he went down through the opening with an acre of silent faces in the street tilted up to watch him. He climbed into the body of the wagon and was seen to bend over the body of Peyton. Then he stood up.

"Is Doc Brown here?"

A fat man pushed through the crowd and laid his hands on the edge of the wagon.

"Take this boy, doc," said the sheriff, "and do what you can for him." The words carried distinctly up and down the length of the crowd.

"All right," said the doctor cheerily. "I'd as soon take care of a hoss thief as another. A case is a case."

"Who called Jerry Peyton a hoss thief?" the sheriff asked. He spoke gently, but once more his voice carried to the outermost edges of the crowd. "What fool called Jerry Peyton a hoss thief?"

No one answered; the six brave men on the steps remained tongue-tied.

Then Doctor Brown said: "Well, I'll be hanged!"

"Take this wagon back to Jerry's place and half a dozen of you put him to bed," the sheriff ordered. "Doc, you stay with him." He turned and went up the steps and opened the door to the jail. "Come in, boys," he said, "I reckon I got room for you all in here."

They looked at one another; then they met the smile

of the sheriff, and finally they trooped in single file through the door.

"Let me understand this," Jan van Zandt said, when they all stood in Sturgis' office. "You stick up for a thief—a hoss thief, Sheriff?" His voice rose as he remembered something from a book. "You want to arrest us because we handled a crook? I tell you to look out, Sturgis. Maybe we didn't have no warrant for what we done; but we taught a lesson that was needed. And we don't need a warrant, because we're the voice of the people."

"You're the voice of a coyote," the sheriff replied sternly. "I recognize it by the whine. Don't talk back to me, Jan. Don't even look back to me. Don't none of the rest of you do nothin' but smile pleasant at me. All of you sit quiet like little lambs, which you are. Don't none of you stir a hand nor raise a head, because I'm plumb fed up. I'm fed up so much that I'm puffin' inside and I'm lookin' for action."

He methodically made a cigarette and lighted it.

"Speakin' of hosses," he said nonchalantly, "they's a chestnut hoss lying in the woods up in Dogberry Canyon. It's been run through the temple with a knife because the hoss give out and the gent that stole him wanted to get rid of all that useless hossflesh. Maybe you'd like to see that hoss, Jan?"

The farmer dropped his head into his hands and groaned. At another time such grief, and particularly for a horse, would have moved the sheriff, but now he let his eyes rest fondly upon Jan through a long moment, and then moved them lingeringly across five other faces.

"Well, boys," he said, "I think I've changed my mind.

I ain't goin' to jail you, and they's a sad reason why. Jerry Peyton is goin' to get well."

The six quivered under the stroke. Jan van Zandt raised his head and gasped.

"And when he gets well," said the sheriff sadly, "he'll be callin' on you to pay you some attentions. He's like the rest of the Peytons. He's like his father. He's thoughtful. I seen his wrists. It'll be four weeks, near, before he can handle a gun. Well, boys, I guess that's all. I wish you all four weeks of good luck."

Jan van Zandt parted his lips to speak.

The sheriff leaped straight into the air, and, coming down, smashed his fist upon the desk. "Not a word out of you, you sneakin', man-slaughterin' coyote. Git out, you and your pack!"

The six, in the same silence, rose and put on their hats, and slunk through the door and silently down the steps to the street. There they parted and the sheriff from a window watched them split apart and travel in different directions. After he had seen this, he turned and took his way through the office to the little wing of the jail where the prisoners were kept.

There was only one man there; the sheriff took his way down the little corridor between the bars of tool-proof steel and the wall. He sat down on a folding stool which leaned close to the bars, and while he rolled another cigarette he looked with interest upon Pat Langley behind the bars.

The latter lay in a vest and stockinged feet on his bunk, and though he was immediately aware that another person had come, it was some time before he laid down his newspaper.

The sheriff spoke first. "I got some news that'll interest you," he said.

Pat Langley yawned deliberately. "Yes?"

"You mostly remember what I said the farmers would do to Jerry Peyton?"

"Is that his name?"

"Old Hank's son." The prisoner whistled.

"Well, they done it," said the sheriff.

"Strung him up, eh?" said Pat Langley, losing interest. "Did he pot any of them?"

"They must of got him when he didn't have a gun," said the sheriff. "They all had the signature of his fist, right enough. I could of told from a block away that they'd been talkin' to Jerry by the look of their faces. I disremember when it was I seen him arguin' with four Mexicans in the street one day."

"Does he make those boys his meat?" Pat Langley asked scornfully.

"Mostly he don't pay no attention to 'em," said the sheriff. "But sometimes he gets his feet all tangled up in 'em, and then he just cuts his way out."

"In self-defense?" inquired Langley.

"Sure," grinned the sheriff. "Otherwise I'd of arrested him long ago, wouldn't I?"

"Of course," said Langley, smiling in turn. They seemed to understand one another perfectly.

"But comin' back to the Mexicans," went on Sturgis, "they was all a husky crew and they took him with a rush while his back was turned and his hands was full of the makin's. It was a pretty sight to foller, if your eyes was fast enough to see all that happened. I disremember, as I was saying, most of the details, but toward the end I recall Jerry steppin' on the face of one of them, while he belted another of them in the jaw. Pretty soon he come up to the door of the jail; he had all the Mexicans tied together. 'I hear you been havin' dull times in your boardin' house,' says he to me. 'So I been drummin' up some trade for you.' And then I got a good look at the faces of them Mexicans, and their own mothers wouldn't of recognized 'em.

"Well, that's the way the six farmers looked today," concluded the sheriff.

"But they hung him, eh?" said Pat, rising upon one elbow to listen.

"Nope."

Pat stretched himself out again, yawning.

"They only hung him up by the wrists," said the sheriff, "to make him confess, I guess. His arms are sure a rotten mess to look at just now. They hung him up till he fainted dead away. Did you ever hear of such foolishness?"

"Foolishness?" Pat questioned.

"Sure, to hang him up and then let him get away alive. Damned foolishness. And now," continued the sheriff, "what'll happen when the boy is on his feet and shoots Jan van Zandt full of holes?"

"Why, when that happens," said the man of the black mustache, "you'll have to go out and get Jerry Peyton." He sat up and laughed. "By heavens, I hadn't thought of that!"

"You got an ugly laugh, Pat," the sheriff said.

"When I read of your demise," said Pat, "I'll give you a tender thought, Ed. But do you know that this terrible Peyton of yours interests me? I wasn't a bad man in a pinch in the old days."

"I'll tell a man," said the sheriff gently.

"And now," went on Pat Langley, "I feel a lot better. As a matter of fact, Ed, it was pretty clever of you not to try a hand-to-hand scrap of it out there in Dogberry Canyon. How did you tell I was in shape?"

"By your hands," said the sheriff. "The rest of you is

pretty fat, but your hands is as skinny and quick as they ever were." He stared fixedly at Pat Langley.

"Well," said Pat, "what do you see—me in a suit of stripes or yourself eating Peyton's lead?"

The little animal eyes of the sheriff went up and down. "D'you know, Pat, that I got a funny thing to tell you?"

"You're full of funny sayings," said the horse thief coldly.

"There you go," murmured the sheriff. "You always have tried to read my mind, Pat, and you always have read it wrong."

There was something sad about the voice of the sheriff that made the other man frown at him.

"Out with it," he said. "What's the funny little thing?"

"Well, ever since I laid eyes on you out in the road up there, I been tryin' to convince myself that I hate you, Pat, but I don't convince worth a cuss."

10

As for Langley, he rolled off the bunk and coming to the steel bars of his cage he took two of them in his small, strong hands and looked steadily through the intervening space at the sheriff. He contented himself with that long, steady gaze, never saying a word. The sheriff blinked once or twice, but, aside from that, he met Langley with a sad, calm regard.

"For instance," said the sheriff, "when I brung you in, I went down to write the charge agin' you onto the little hotel register that I keep for my guests. Well, somehow I couldn't write down the number that means larceny after your name. Couldn't do it, Pat. I couldn't even write down your name.

"Are you playing a little game?" asked Langley, and he pressed his face against the bars in his desire to look through the little eyes of Ed Sturgis and get at his mind.

"Me?" queried the other in surprise. "What sort of a game do I need to play on you now, Pat?"

It was quite unanswerable. This truth gradually became clear in the mind of Langley.

"I can even explain why you feel this way," he said with a sudden change of voice.

"You was always a great hand at explainin'," murmured the sheriff, but though Pat Langley shot one of his sudden glances at Sturgis he was able to read nothing in the bland face of his old companion.

"This is why," Pat said. "In the old days I did you a great wrong, Ed. You have kept that in mind all these years, you see. You've been hating me all this time and wishing and waiting for a chance to get back at me. Is that the truth?"

"I guess it's pretty close to gospel, old-timer."

"But down in your heart," continued Pat Langley, "all the time, you weren't hating me so much as the thing I had done."

The sheriff blinked again. "I don't quite follow," he murmured.

"I mean this," Pat said hurriedly. "Outside of that one thing I did, I was always square with you. I played straight. I backed you up in every pinch. You remember?"

"That's true."

"So all these twenty years," said Langley, "you've been concentrating to hate that one thing I did. It was a mean piece of work. I don't deny that, Ed, and not once during these years have I attempted to excuse it to myself."

"Go on," said the sheriff, and a little spot of white had come in either cheek. "Let's leave that go."

"Let that pass." Langley nodded. "And when you saw me today it was a man you couldn't recognize. You found that you didn't hate that stranger you met in the road. It wasn't until you found out his name that you began to hate him. Is that straight, Eddie?"

It must have been to conceal his emotion that the sheriff looked down and placed his hand above his eyes. He was thinking, and it was some time before he could raise his head and look at his prisoner again. When he did so, it was to say: "Pat, you're right."

The other turned, and since he dared not raise his voice and, above all, allow the sheriff to see his face, he turned and walked to his bunk and stood with his back to the sheriff and his head fallen.

"What's the matter?" asked the sheriff cheerily, after a time.

"It's because I can't help thinking what a rotten thing I did," Pat Langley said, choking. "And you—Ed—when all's done, you were the finest friend I've ever had."

"Tut, tut," the sheriff replied. "D'you mean that?"

"Do you doubt me?" cried Langley, whirling on his heel. "Now that I'm here and down and ruined—do you doubt me?" He waved to the bars, to the wretched bunk.

"Yes," agreed the sheriff, "sometimes the steel slats work through the blankets and sort of leave a pattern on a gent's back. Them bunks ain't what I'd recommend to anybody that likes to lie soft at night."

To this naive speech the reply of the horse thief was another of the flickering, bright glances; but there was apparently no mockery in the face of the sheriff.

"What I'm chiefly sorry for," said Langley, "is that I've left you in another mess by this unfortunate episode of the chestnut horse."

"Yep," agreed the sheriff, "that's a pretty bad mix-up, all right. Tell me, honest, Pat, did you figure on sending back the price of that hoss when you got to the end of your trip?"

"So help me, I did!" Langley said, and there was a ring of truth in his voice.

"My, my," said the sheriff. "You have changed a pile, Pat. Well, I'll tell you about this Peyton. I tell you I fear him, and I do. You remember his dad, don't you?"

"Old Hank? Of course, I had a run-in with him, you remember."

"And came out on top. Yes, I remember. But Hank was a fast man and pretty accurate, and his son is a shade better. But why I fear him is because he has all my luck. No use runnin' foul of a man that has your luck."

"How did he get it?" said Pat Langley, with interest. "To tell you the truth, Ed, you're a fool to fear any man under thirty. It takes a certain age to harden a man's nerve, and the boy could never stand up to you."

"Not unless he had my luck, I wouldn't bat an eye about him."

"H-m-m," Langley said. "That makes a difference, of course."

"It was just before I come to Sloan," the sheriff continued. "First place I landed when I went west was in Nevada, and I hit her when she was wide open and roarin'."

"I've always regretted missing those days in Nevada." Pat Langley sighed.

"Sure, you would have been right at home," agreed the sheriff.

Again Langley looked to discover proof of a double meaning, but he found nothing.

"I was some green," the sheriff went on, "in those days. I was all set up to find trouble. Knew how to shoot, I thought, and at a target I was some handy boy.

So I got all togged up with a brace of gats and a frosty eye and went about with a chip on my shoulder. Particular, I had one gun that was a beauty. It was a new model, just out of the shop, and she worked like she had brains of her own. In fact, it's a pretty old model for a Colt today, but in fingers that know their business it don't have to take a back seat to nothin' right up to this minute."

"I think I know that old model," said Pat.

"With that gun," the sheriff continued, "I felt like Hercules, and then some. And so one evenin' I run into a little gent in a saloon. We was playin' cards and I seen him palm a card once; then I seen him do it again. For that matter, they was a couple of the other boys that I was sure had seen it, but they didn't say nothin'. At the time, I wondered why; but I didn't stop to ask any questions about who this gent was. I just give him a call and then start for my gun. Well, Pat, he got me covered before I had my forefinger on the butt of my gun.

"He seen I was a kid and mostly fool though, and he didn't feel much like action, I guess. Anyway, he let me off with a bit of advice, and he took away both my guns for safekeepin', he said, to keep me out of trouble."

"Funny you never told me this story before," Langley said.

"When I knew you," said the sheriff, "I was still too young. The thing was too fresh in my mind, and I hadn't reached the stage when I could tell about the lickin's I'd had in the past. Now, I can grin about 'em."

"H-m-m," Langley said thoughtfully.

"But the point of that yarn ain't out yet. The name of the quiet gent that got my guns was La Paloma."

"The devil you say," murmured Langley.

"The devil I do say," said the sheriff calmly. "It was

sure La Paloma, though he hadn't picked up that name yet, and that gun he got from me was the one he always packed later on. That's the gun the Mexicans called the Voice of La Paloma, he used it so handy."

"But what the devil has that to do with your luck leaving you, Ed?"

"Why just this: The chap that got La Paloma—that was two years after you left—was Hank Peyton, you see? And Hank got the Voice of La Paloma and passed it along to his kid. So Jerry has my gun; and who ever had any luck trailin' a gent that had your own gun? It's more'n that, Pat. The kid puts an awful lot of stock in that gun. I figure he ain't practiced with anything else since he was knee-high, and if he didn't have it he'd be up in the air. You see how everything turns around it? He's got my luck. My luck is his luck. There you are, and when Jerry Peyton bumps off the first of them farmers—I wish to heaven that he'd get the whole crew of 'em at once, for my part! I got to go out on the trail of a gent that has all my luck pulling at his holster. I'd as soon jump over a cliff. I wouldn't be no surer of dyin' that way."

As he concluded this gloomy story, the sheriff's eyes dropped to the floor and remained there, studying the shadow. It gave Pat Langley a chance to lift his own glance and observe every detail of the face of the other man. He even permitted the faintest hint of a smile which might have been either contempt or scorn to touch his lips. Then he brushed his smile away and came close to the bars.

"Ed," he whispered.

"Well, Pat," the sheriff said absently.

"I have a little proposition which might interest you."

"Fire away, old-timer."

"You say you haven't put my name in the book?"

"I haven't."

"And no one knows that I'm here?"

"Not a soul." He looked quickly into Pat Langley's face. "What are you figurin' on, Pat?"

"On playing your game and mine with the same hand, old boy."

"Go on, Pat. You was always a hand at sayin' surprisin' things."

"Ed, you've already admitted that your old grudge against me is dead. I'm simply a burden on your hands here. Well, let me out of this mess. Give me a horse and a gun. I'll doll myself up in a mask and slide over to the house of this young Peyton—do the robber stunt, you see? Turn things upside down, and finally take his gun and bring it out to you. Then you'll have your luck back and I'll have my freedom and a horse to go on my way. What d'you think?"

"I can't think," the sheriff said. "Gimme air!"

11

It was on the second night following this that the sheriff and Pat Langley rode out of Sloan and took the way down the valley. They cut across the fields, and came by a generous detour behind the house and farm buildings of Jerry Peyton. They had the clear mountain, starlike, to guide them, and even by that dull light they made out the dilapidated outbuildings; there were broken gang plows and worn-out two-horse rakes standing about, silent tokens of Jerry's complete failure as a farmer.

They dismounted beside a big barn, and when they passed the open door they could see the stars through gaps of the roof. The big haymow was empty; and the long row of stalls on either side of the mow contained not a single horse or even a mule. Pat Langley noted this and shrugged his shoulders.

"Makes me feel like the devil," he muttered to the

sheriff. "Hate to see a place go to ruin. I remember when the Peyton place was a comfortable little farm. Old Mrs. Peyton was a wonderful cook, too; and now look at her kitchen!"

That wing of the house presented a roof which sagged far in.

"You got a tenderness for houses that you never used to have," commented the sheriff. "Maybe that comes out of the coin you've made in St. Hilaire."

The other made no answer; he was taking stock of the place rapidly.

"I don't see your point in not giving me a gun with teeth in it," he said angrily to the sheriff. "Suppose that young devil in there can use either one of his hands—he'll punch me full of lead when I shove this empty bunch of iron junk in his face."

"He can't raise an arm, let alone handle a gun," said the sheriff. "He can't even feed himself. The neighbors have to come in and take care of him like a baby."

"Ah, that's it! Then I'll have some of these handy neighbors about when I slip in?"

"Not a one. They've left before now."

The sheriff felt the discontented glance of the horse thief through the starlight.

"I leave it to you to warn me in case anyone comes," said Pat Langley.

"The old sign," said the sheriff. "You can depend upon that."

"Well, here goes," and lifting his hat a little, a curtain of absolute dark rushed over the dim face of Langley.

The sheriff whispered: "Are you nervous, Pat?"

"Nonsense," answered the other. "Nervous? I'm enjoying every minute of it!"

"And it won't bother you none to go in there and take that kid's gun away from him?"

"Why should it?" Langley retorted.

His tone had changed since the mask covered his face; in fact, there was a new atmosphere around the two men.

"I mean, him bein' helpless," murmured the sheriff. "It won't make you feel like a skunk to take his gun away when he ain't got a fightin' chance, will it?"

The other chuckled almost silently. "Listen to me, old boy. I left my scruples back in St. Hilaire. This is a party for me. S'long!" And he disappeared around the side of the house.

The sheriff, after a moment, made a few steps in pursuit, but then he came back to the horses and stood at their heads, lest something in the night should make one of them whinny. He began to rub his pinto's nose nervously, and to whisper into the ear of Langley's horse. Yet there was not a sound from the direction of the house.

Once the thought came to the sheriff that Langley might give over the attempt to rob Peyton and go away into the night, but on second thought he knew that the other would not risk an escape on foot. The horses caught the man's wish for silence and stood without stirring as they listened into the night. Then something that was not a sound made the sheriff turn; he saw his companion once more at his shoulder.

They swung into the saddle without another word and headed across the fields at a trot; as soon as a comfortable distance lay behind them, they let their horses have their heads and went at a wild gallop; halfway back to Sloan they stopped of one accord.

"Well?" the sheriff asked.

The other ripped away his mask and tore it into a hundred shreds; then he tossed the balled-up remnants into the dust.

"Not so simple as you'd think," Langley said. He shrugged his shoulders to get rid of some thought. "He's a bad one well enough, that young Peyton."

"Made a try for you?"

"Oh, no. He sat in his chair and couldn't lift a hand, just as you said, but he got on my nerves. Can you imagine a fellow who sits perfectly still and follows you with his eyes while you run through his stuff?"

"I can," said the sheriff, and for some reason his voice carried a world of meaning.

"The kid was cool enough," said the other. "I went through his wallet—it was in the table drawer. 'Help yourself,' says young Peyton. Cheery smile he has, isn't it?"

"Yep. He's a fine-lookin' gent."

"I took the coin. Only twenty bucks, at that, but it would have looked queer if I hadn't taken it. I told him I was sorry to do it, though; but being broke—he just nodded at me. 'That's all right,' he says."

"Ah," sighed the sheriff. "You spoke to him?" He did not seem displeased.

"Of course," said Langley. "But he changed his tune when I came to his gun rack. I ran through the stuff and found the Voice of La Paloma. Rum name for a gun, eh? I knew it by the make and by the nicks that were filed into the butt. 'Just a minute,' says the kid. 'You don't really want that gun, I guess.'

"'Why don't I?' I said.

"'You don't understand,' says the kid. 'That gun used to belong to my father. It means a good deal to me.

The gun you want is the new Colt that hangs next to the old pump-gun.'

"'Don't jolly yourself along,' I said to him. 'I know the make of a gun, and this suits me to a T.'

"For a minute I thought I'd have a bit of trouble even with that handless man; he leaned forward in his chair. 'You shouldn't do that!' he said. 'Don't take that gun!' From the way he spoke, I had a ghost of an idea that he had twenty men behind his chair ready to grab me. I had to blink at him, and his face wasn't pretty. 'If you're so set on it,' I said, 'I'll leave the money, but I've got to have this little cannon.'

"'Then,' says friend Jerry, 'you're a fool.'

"'So?' I said to him.

"'Because if you take the coin, and anything else you see here, I'll let it go. But if you take that gun I'll follow you.'

"You won't believe that it gave me a chill to hear him say it? You know me, Ed?"

"I know you well enough," said the sheriff dryly, "but I believe you got the chill."

"I did, all right. 'How'll you get my trail?' I asked the kid. 'You don't know me. If you live to be a hundred you'll never know my name, and you'll never see my face. Tell me how you'll follow me, partner?'

"He didn't bat an eye. If he knew anything, you'd think he'd keep still about it, eh? Not Jeremiah. He came right out with it in a way that didn't particularly help my nerves. 'I know your height,' he says; 'I know your weight; I know you have black hair with a touch of gray in it and you're about forty-five years old; you have a heavy mustache—the mask bulges out around your mouth; and your eyes are black. More than that, I know your voice and I know your hands. Those hands

alone would give me a clue. They'll leave a sign I can
follow. So take my advice, partner, and put that gun
back in the case, because, if you take it, I give you my
word of honor that I'll never rest or draw a free breath
till I've run you down and killed you.'

"That was a mouthful for a helpless kid to say to me,
when I had a bead on him, eh? I don't ask you to
believe it, but just for a minute I had a feeling that I'd
like to tell you to go hang, put the gun in the case, and
take a chance on running across country on foot. Of
course I didn't do what I felt like doing. And here's the
Voice of La Paloma."

He extended the old revolver, and the sheriff took it
and bent his head over it; then he balanced it in his
hand.

"Seems like I still recognize it," he said.

He examined it, made sure that it was loaded, and
then turned the muzzle full upon his companion.

"Now," he said, "sit tight and listen to me while I
talk."

The other stared. "Well, I'll be—" he murmured.

"Easy, friend," interrupted the sheriff. "Don't move
that gun out of your holster. Good!"

"What's got into your crazy head," said Pat Langley
after a moment, "is more than I can make out. If you're
going to double-cross me, go ahead, I'm not fool enough
to make a break when you have a bead on me. Want my
hands up?"

"No. Do whatever you want with 'em, and use your
ears to listen to what I've got to say. I didn't know you
then, Pat, but the minute I heard about the way you
run a knife into that hoss, it turned me agin' you. And
after that, I didn't like the way you tried to bribe me,

Pat. Still, I didn't see how low-down mean you could be till later on."

Langley sat with his head canted, nodding. "It's odd," he said, "that an intelligent man like you, Ed, can live nearly fifty years without increasing his vocabulary. Go ahead."

"No, I ain't clever, Pat. But I was clever enough to see that I was in a mess on account of you stealin' the hoss and Peyton gettin' beat up for the same thing. I saw Peyton make his kill after his wrists got well; I saw him go plumb wild; I saw Sheriff Sturgis go out to get him and get drilled full of lead tryin' to do it.

"You see, I ain't clever, Pat, but I seen all that, and I thought I'd see if I couldn't make a combination and get out of trouble. Here you were in jail. If I got bumped off I could hear you laugh. There was Peyton, getting well for a scrap later on. I wondered if I couldn't get rid of both of you. Well, I played stupid. You bein' a clever gent, I just gave you a lead, and you worked it all out for me. The lead I give you was that cock and bull yarn about the Voice of La Paloma. Pat, I thought you were sure fooling me when I saw you swallow that yarn."

Langley nodded again. "I begin to see light," he said calmly.

"Still," went on the sheriff, "I didn't see my way clear out until you told me yourself that you'd make the dirty bargain. You'd go out and take that gun from a kid that couldn't help himself. Honest, though, Pat, I hated to think they was such a yellow-hearted skunk in the world as you are! But you done it. You made the plan and then you went right ahead and took the gun. And now, partner, you're fixed. Far as I'm concerned, you're free. I got no holts on you. You can ride as far as you please. As far as the kid is concerned, I'm rid of him, too. He ain't goin' to do no killin' in my county. No, sir. He'll hop on a hoss as soon as he gets well, and he'll never think of nothin' until he finds his dad's gun ag'in and gets it back."

"I see," said Langley coldly. "You'll point out the way to St. Hilaire to him?"

"I'd ought to, I guess," said the sheriff, with a sigh. "But I won't. I like to see a rabbit get a fair start before a hound catches him. Well, Pat, I give you a start off from here to St. Hilaire, and you better use it; because water ain't goin' to stop young Peyton when he hits the trail. He'll nose you out, old boy, and he'll finish you, a long ways off from Sloan."

"He's free to follow," Langley said. "If the young fool is keen enough to trail me to the West Indies from the border, I'll almost regret that I have to shoot him. But, in conclusion, I have to admit that you've improved your method since the old days, Ed. You were always a bit of a coward when it came to facing me, but in those times you hadn't enough brains to think of sending a substitute after me. So long, old boy.

"Well," called the sheriff after him, "I kind of expected you'd get in the last word. Ride hard, Pat."

12

Doctor Brown, besides attending to his patient, kept six anxious farmers apprised of his condition through daily bulletins which were followed with painful interest by the farmers and their wives and children. Their relatives, also, came to read the bulletins of Doctor Brown. With groans of distress they noted the day on which the doctor sent word that his patient was for the first time able to use a spoon, and later still that he was able to work with a very sharp knife and put enough pressure on the edge to cut his own meat.

That was gloomy news to the six. Without waiting longer Pierre la Roche sold his farm, packed his belongings, and huddled wife and family aboard a train headed for parts unknown.

Then came the day when it was known that the bandages had been finally removed from the wrists of the sufferer and it was only a matter of time before he would have complete use of his fingers and arm muscles.

These terrible tidings swept Pete Goodwin and Eric Jensen and Gus Saunders out of Sloan and carried them away to parts as unknown as those which had received the family of la Roche. There still remained Rex Houlahan and Jan van Zandt. Rex held out until Doctor Brown reported that the big cowpuncher was exercising every day, and that his exercise consisted largely in faithful practice with weapons. Then Rex Houlahan disappeared from the ken of man.

The sheriff rubbed his hands together, and that night he slept well for the first time in six weeks, but when the morning came he found that Jan van Zandt still remained. It troubled the sheriff, this incredible stupidity. He went out and told the prospective martyr some homely truths about himself, but Jan van Zandt merely stared at the sheriff and grew a little whiter about the mouth; he refused to leave.

The other farmers formed what might be called a protective association, but for some reason they failed to invite Jan to join. Indeed, no one wanted to be seen in his company, or to pose as his friend. Over Sloan and all the valley lay the fear of Jeremiah.

The creditors, at about this time, hurried affairs along. They foreclosed, and the shuddering population of Sloan were informed that out of the sale young Peyton had secured only enough funds to buy for himself a fine new revolver, a reliable horse, an outfit of clothes, and food suitable for a long and hasty trip on horseback.

On the next day he took a room in the hotel. On the day after that the doctor let it be known that his patient was completely restored. On the following day, the friends and relatives of Jan van Zandt came to call upon him, pressed his hand, muttered a word of farewell, and left him hurriedly.

And the morning after that, Sloan wakened with astonishment to learn that Peyton was gone from their midst, whither no man knew, and that Jan van Zandt still drew the breath of life!

The sheriff collapsed when he heard the news, and then he set about hunting for the clues. All he could learn was that young Peyton had made inquiries about a man in the neighborhood of forty-five years of age, a hundred and seventy pounds in weight, five feet and ten inches in height, black hair, and bright, black eyes, and a heavy mustache. He had appeared interested in Sid Ruben's account of a man who answered that description. Sid had passed him in Dogberry Canyon on the way toward Tannerville, apparently. The sheriff ran inadvertently upon this unimportant bit of news; he was observed to go back to his office singing, a little later, and before the day was over Jerry Peyton was forgotten in the routine of Sloan's busy life.

The town of Sloan was forgotten by Jeremiah Peyton even more completely. Between his knees he had a mud-colored gelding whose savage eye had pleased him long ago in the corral of Sam Wetherby; in his holster was a gun which had fitted into the palm of his hand like the grip of an old friend; on his feet were shop-made boots, at forty dollars; on his heels jingled new spurs; around his neck was a bandanna handkerchief of the finest silk and of a screaming crimson; in his pocket a wallet bulged more or less comfortably; between his fingers the reins slipped to and fro as he kept the feel of the mustang's head; and in his heart was the glorious knowledge that he was free!

The mud-colored gelding carried all that he owned in the world; there was no weight of possessions to take him back to any place; he was like a ship with anchors cut away, blowing for a distant port as he galloped down Dogberry Canyon that morning, and he felt as a sailor, long landlocked, feels when a deck heaves under his heels again, and the wind cuts into his face.

The stranger with the small, white, agile hands was his goal; there were other ports which he must touch before the voyage ended, Pierre la Roche, Jan van Zandt, and the others, but he pushed these into the background of his mind. He had an oath which would keep his helm steadily toward the man of the mask and carry by all the others until that port was reached.

He had picked up one more important detail, the color of the horse on which the stranger rode when he left Sloan, and with that added fact, he had little trouble in picking up another step of the trail at Tannerville. No one remembered the man with the white hands, it seemed, saving Dick Jerkin, the gambler. He had sat in with this man, it appeared. The stranger had given his name as Owen Peyne and he played a stiff game of poker. Dick dropped a couple of hundred in an hour's play and was about to lose more, according to the luck, when a fortunate call dragged him away from this expert, who seemed to read the cards.

So far the trail was simple, for in the direction of Dogberry Canyon, Tannerville was almost the only stop out of Sloan, but beyond Tannerville the towns multiplied. Jerry cast a circle around Tannerville and after three days of hard riding and much talk he came on the clue again.

This time the name of the stranger was Bert Morgan, and Peyton smiled when he heard it, for it proved that the man with the agile hands had remembered the threat which Jeremiah spoke; now he was covering his trail.

It was in the town of Benton that Jerry found the trail again and beyond Benton, of course, lies a wilderness; so Jerry cast a line from Tannerville to Benton, and projecting the line straight ahead, he struck into the desert and went by compass.

The compass brought him into a jerkwater town a hundred and fifty miles from Benton, and in this town of Lancaster the sign of the stranger completely disappeared. No one had ever heard of either Morgan or Peyne; no one knew of a rather stocky man with graystreaked hair and a heavy mustache who spent money freely and gambled for high stakes. So Peyton, in despair, vented some pent-up wrath on a restaurant which served him a stale tamale, and leaving a wreck behind him he went on across the desert, somewhat soothed.

The stranger had not been in Lancaster; therefore either Lancaster was peopled by fools who could not remember, or else the stranger, also striving to leave a difficult trail, had skipped this link in his journey. So it seemed to Jerry, and traveling still by compass, he went for three more days across the desert until he reached a town which consisted of a crossroads store and three shacks.

There they knew neither Morgan nor Peyne, but they were very much acquainted with a gentleman named Harry Wister, who had left one staggering wreck of a horse, bought another regardless of price, and then shot off into the desert again. All this was six weeks before, and Peyton thrilled through every long hard muscle when he thought of the speed of the stranger. For a holdup man he was a most unusual criminal; he squandered money like a drunken millionaire; and he rode like a demon.

In Sandy Waters he found news of the second change of horses and a white-handed gentleman named Peters; six weeks ago he had gone through, with a two-hour stop. By this time Jerry had heard the face of the man described so often that he almost knew the well-fed cheeks and the bright eyes, and the white teeth which showed when he smiled. Then, five hundred miles from Tannerville, he reached the western and northern limit of the trail. It went out as completely as if the stranger had ridden into running water.

To say that Peyton was discouraged would be to put it far too mildly; but when a man has worked for thirty days at one affair he will not give it up too lightly. Peyton took out his spite in a street fight. These affairs with fists were something he rarely indulged in, but bumping up against a bunch of half-drunken, savage Scandinavians gave him his chance. It was from every angle a glorious affair.

For half an hour the ears of Jerry were filled with a roar of strong language volleyed at him from five mouths. They were all strong men; even when they fell they would catch at him and almost drag him down, and Jerry had fought like a wolf among dogs, leaping and striking and leaping clear. At length, with one eye closed, Jerry shook himself to make sure that he was still holding together, cast one glance at the five disfigured Danes, and then staggered into the little hotel, content.

He slept for twenty-four hours after that. The deputy sheriff, who came to make inquiries about the fight, looked at Jerry as he lay asleep, went through his belongings, and then left, declaring that a man who could sleep more than twelve hours had a clear conscience.

The Danes, though beaten, were not altogether discouraged. They mustered their forces, and as soon as Jerry was out of sight of the town, they gave him a flying start on his journey back to the south and east; but Jerry was feeling too happy to be vindictive. He shot horses instead of men, and when the informal posse had melted away, he went blithely on his course.

He had before him ten days of riding in circles from town to town; and then, at last, he came upon no less a hero of the green-topped table than "Snowy" Garrison. Snowy had come across Jeremiah years before, when Jerry was hardly more than a boy, except to those who knew him, and after a slight falling out, they had shaken hands and departed, one from the other, sworn friends.

On this second meeting, Snowy was bulging with prosperity. He had a suite of rooms in the hotel—for this was Chambers City—and a boy to call him in the morning and put him to bed at night. Also he had a roll of money that choked his valise.

To Jerry he imparted the tale of a stranger who had come to Chambers City with a bright smile and agile fingers. Of how the stranger had gathered three stable citizens together and taken their money with oiled ease, extracting the savings of years painlessly. Then he, Snowy Garrison, proposing a game, was struck dumb to find a man who knew neither his name nor his widespread repute. His nerves were so shaken by thus discovering the meagerness of mortal fame that he straightway lost three thousand dollars in three gloomy minutes.

The play of the stranger finally recalled him to his better self, and, at twelve o'clock sharp, the stranger declared that his cash was gone and wished to know if a check would be acceptable. Snowy then peered at the well-fed cheeks of the stranger and declared that a check would be a very acceptable tribute.

So they continued to play until dawn; and the next day Snowy found himself in possession of a series of little yellow slips of paper, each with:

"James P. Langley, St. Hilaire, W. I.," written across the back, and every check was upon a New York bank.

"And when I put 'em in for collection," added Snowy Garrison, "darned if they didn't get cashed in—all of 'em!"

"Some millionaire out for an airing, maybe," said Jerry. "Well, if I had the kale that some of those gents have, I'd get as close to nature as I want in Central Park."

"You're talking for us both," declared Snowy with emotion.

"But what did he look like, this fellow?" said Jerry, who had fallen into the habit of asking about the personal appearance of everyone since he took this empty trail.

"Middle-aged, middle height, medium weight," said Snowy, "but what I noticed first was his hands. They was so small and white, you see?"

Long, lean fingers closed over the wrist of Snowy and burned the flesh against the bones with their grip.

"Spit it out," said Jerry, "was his hair black?"

13

Information was not all that Jerry obtained through Snowy Garrison; he also sat in at an honest game of blackjack, with Jerry's forty-five in view on a nearby chair to discourage any tricks from Snowy. The honest game replenished Jerry's pocketbook, so that, the following morning, he found himself aboard a train with two tickets to New Orleans, an entire compartment for himself, and a bottle of yellow Old Crow.

His first impulse was to open his wallet, and in it he discovered more money than he had ever seen there before; accordingly, hearing voices outside the compartment—for Jerry had never ridden in a Pullman before— he summoned the speakers by beating upon the metal door with the butt of his gun. The voices outside stopped; and then a porter popped his head to see how matters stood.

From him Jerry ascertained a few details from the

blank of his memory. He learned that he had appeared in the train with a companion, both hatless and without luggage. He discovered that his companion had wept feelingly over him, placed twenty dollars in the hand of the porter, and assured him that he must put his dear brother, Mr. Jerry Peyton, off the train at New Orleans, where he'd take a ship to St. Hilaire.

It was from this porter, also, that Jerry learned many other important facts which influenced his future. He heard that in St. Hilaire people would probably be wearing white at this time of the year, and that spurs, in that island, would be an unnecessary part of his outfit. So when the train reached New Orleans, Jerry outfitted himself in whites and bought his first pair of canvas low-cut shoes, a straw hat so flexible that it could be rolled up and put inside a little cane tube, and a ticket for St. Hilaire.

In due time, having passed through a season of white-hot sea and then a sea whipped by a hurricane, Jerry found himself seated on the veranda of the American consul's house at St. Hilaire, growing acquainted with a pungent gin disguised in little glasses of milk and getting the feel of a new air.

The consul's house sat on the brow of a little hill with its face toward the sea, "and it's back on St. Hilaire, thank heaven!" as the consul said shortly after Jerry had presented the bottle of Old Crow to him.

At this Jerry stood up and, looking down the length of the side veranda, he could see all of the town of St. Hilaire. Five big hills, like five stubby fingers, went up beyond the town, shutting out the view of the rest of the island, and St. Hilaire lay in the palm of the hand. At first glance it appeared to be merely a smear of green—a bright, shining green such as Jerry had never seen before—

but presently he discovered under the trees a number of little houses which followed the course of streets.

They were not streets laid down with any plan. They must have been constructed by engineers who worked on the system of cattle making a path, and, weaving heedlessly from side to side, following always the low ground. If Jerry had taken a coil of rope, shaken it loose, and flung it sprawling in the dust, the pattern it left would have been a fair representation of the plan of St. Hilaire. Looking more closely, Jerry could see some of the houses quite distinctly, particularly a few on the edge of the town nearest him, and he saw that the slant light of the sun shone quite through them. They were more like lean-tos thrown up for the night than lifelong habitations.

"Still," said Jerry, "I kind of like the color of that green stuff, and, speaking personal, if I were to own this house of yours, I don't think I'd sit out facing the sea."

He apparently struck a vital spark in the consul with this last remark.

"Color?" said the consul. He started to stand up in turn, but changing his mind he merely sat forward in his chair and waved generously along the shore line of the bay.

It was a graceful little harbor, an almost perfect horseshoe, with one spot of white in the center where the waves smashed into foam on a bit of coral reef. The points of the horseshoe were low, sandy bars, thrusting out into the sea. The sand was very white, and the consul called Jerry's attention to it.

"It's the sort of white," he declared, "that can't be painted. It's the sort of white that—that a painter uses for the brow of a woman."

At this the cowpuncher gaped, but the consul turned

to him with a broad grin. "Have another drink," he said, pushing the bottle across the table.

The astonishment passed from Jerry's face as the consul kicked an inverted dishpan by way of a gong and bellowed to an agile little Negro for ice.

"Have another drink," said the consul, putting some of the ice into Jerry's glass, and spinning it expertly with a spoon held between two fingers, "and don't mind me."

Jerry accepted the drink, and after he had had it, modified the strength of the remark he had intended making.

"Maybe that white is all right," he said, "but still it's too close to the sea to suit me."

The consul leaned back in his chair, looking first at Jerry and then at the sea, and Jerry was sure that surprising words were about to issue from the consul's lips. He was correct.

"Too close to the sea?" echoed the consul, speaking solemnly. "Why, sir, the sea was placed there by God for the express purpose of bringing out the color of that sand spit. And the white sand spit was placed there by God to bring out the profound blue of the ocean."

He sipped his gin and milk and appeared to contemplate either the picture before him, the gin, or his own remark. He was not more than two years older than Jerry, the latter thought, but his hair was already so gray that it would be silver before long. His face would have been noble had the flesh not puffed a little too much about the eyes; also the eyes, though large, were smeared with mist, and only now and then the vital spark showed through. Jerry was so busy watching that face that he forgot to reply to the last remark of the consul.

"It is, in fact, a composition," the other continued.

"It's a planned bit of work. The sea, the white sand, the sky—you observe—"

"Wait," Jerry interrupted. "I agree with what you say about the sand and the sky, well enough, Mr. Rimshaw, but why the dickens can't you leave out the sea?"

"You object to the sea?" asked the consul sadly.

Jerry scratched his big head and considered.

"The sea," he finally decided, "is like a bucking horse that never hits the ground." Unconsciously he laid a hand upon his stomach. "The sea," he began again, but could say no more.

"The sea," said the consul, in such haste that he drank only half of his glass, "is the only part of nature where the mind of man is free to expand limitlessly. The sea—" he paused in the midst of his exordium, so absentmindedly that Jerry was barely in time to reach across the table and direct the stream of gin which the consul was pouring into his glass instead of upon the floor.

"Say," said Jerry, "maybe you're a painter yourself, in your off hours? Sort of work at it on the side?"

"Sir," the young man said soulfully, "I am an author."

"The devil you are!" cried Jerry, amazed.

"The devil I'm not," repled the other, with some force. "If I'm not an author what would you call the writer of six plays, three novels, and countless essays, short stories, and verses?"

"I'm not arguing," Jerry said calmly. "I'm just wondering. If you're an author, what are you doing down here?"

"Studying human nature in the raw," replied the consul readily.

"Have another drink," Jerry said, pouring out one. "I sure like to hear you talk. In the raw, eh?"

"And waiting to find an intelligent editor," continued

the author. "You'd be surprised, sir, if you knew how cramped the foreheads of our leading editors are. To me, it is shocking."

"Too bad," Jerry said consolingly.

"You can't understand," the author went on, "until you've learned by experience which costs so many pangs of the heart; and so much hard cash spent on paper and postage," he added. "Since I was nine, sir, I have been pouring my heart out on paper, and, after a life of labor, the editorial brain of the English-speaking world condemns me to a hole like St. Hilaire. I ask you, sir, what would you do in a case like mine?"

"Cut out the booze," replied the cowpuncher instantly, "and get into training."

He was astonished to see the author turn sharply in his chair with a broad grin. "That's sound advice," Mr. Rimshaw commented. "After you were in training what would you do?"

"Sir," said Jerry suddenly, stiffening, "I sort of gather that you're smiling."

"Do you?" said the consul.

"Are you smiling with me or at me?" Jerry asked coldly.

There is a certain tone of voice which brings men up standing with as much surety as the rattle of a snake or the snarl of an angry dog.

The consul blinked. "With you, of course," he said soberly.

"I sort of had my doubts, that's all," Jerry replied, and leaning back in his chair, he regarded the author with a hungry eye.

"You were about to give me some advice," the author said.

"Oh, yes. Well, if I were in your boots, I'd grab a

horse—I mean a boat—and I'd buy a through ticket to the dugouts where these editors sit around."

"Ah?" said the author.

"Then," the cowpuncher continued firmly, "I'd go in, with a story under one arm and a gat under the other, and find out what he meant by wastin' my money on postage."

"Do you know what would happen?" questioned the author.

"I got an idea," said Jerry blandly. "What d'you figure?"

"You'd never be able to get in to see the editor!"

"Wouldn't I?" said Jerry. "Well, well!" And he grinned openly at the consul.

"And if you did," said the author, "and started any fancy talk, the editor would have you thrown out."

"Which?" asked Jerry, his eyes widening.

"Thrown out."

"With what?" Jerry queried.

"With their hands," said the consul, frowning at such stupidity, "and they'd speed you on your way with the ends of their boots."

"My, my," said Jerry gently. "They must be rough men."

The consul turned squarely about for the first time. The mist gradually stirred from across his vision and two keen eyes looked squarely into the face of Jerry.

"Well," said the author, "what the devil are you doing down here?"

"I'm just touring about, studying human nature in the raw." Jerry grinned.

"Well," said the consul, "the population of St. Hilaire is about twenty thousand and two, and you'll find about two people that's worth while in the place. One of them is yourself; modesty prevents me from naming the other one."

14

"Simple," said Jerry, "direct, and to the point. But then I'd like to get the gent in Chambers City who hoisted a flag over St. Hilaire and said it was the best island for its weight that ever stepped into the Atlantic."

"Who was the bird?" said the author.

"Name was—what the devil?—I forget. Middle-aged chap with gray hair and glasses."

"Respectable?" asked the consul.

"Sure, I won some money from him."

"And he steered you for St. Hilaire? Well, I'll tell you. If you have the price of a ticket home, grab the next boat."

"H-m-m," said Jerry, stirring the ice about in his glass. "So far St. Hilaire isn't so bad; don't see much wrong with it except the long drive to the gate."

"What did he say about it?"

"Oh, I don't know. Said it was full of trees and people and money."

"What kind of trees?" asked the consul quickly.

"Poker trees," said Jerry, with innocent eyes.

"Ah!" The author grinned. "I see. Well, there are plenty of poker trees. I have one myself that's not so bad. But taking them all in all, the poker trees that you can climb don't produce fruit that's worth picking; and the ones that are worth while are all fenced in."

"I'm some fence climber," Jerry assured him.

"Social fences," the consul and author continued. "Kind of people who give you a cold smile and tea once a year. Oh, this is a devil of a fine place, this St. Hilaire. But speaking of poker, I—"

"How high do you run?" asked Jerry coldly.

"H-m-m," the consul uttered thoughtfully.

"Business is business," said Jerry.

"Oh," the consul replied, "I see. Well, I guess you don't want to talk to me. But I'll give you the layout of the joint. Personally, I'd like to see somebody break down a few boards and get through the fence; maybe some of the rest of us could get through the hole."

"Is it worth while getting through the fences?" asked Jerry.

"Dear, innocent Jerry Peyton," the consul remarked, "is it worth your while? Let me tell you a few facts. There are exactly three hundred and thirteen thousand acres of workable land in St. Hilaire; and the land that can be worked is so rich that all you have to do is sit and smile at it to make things grow. Matter of fact, the hard work is only to make the right things grow. If you can beat the weeds you have a fortune by the throat. Well, this land is cut up about as follows: A hundred and thirteen thousand acres are held by five thousand land owners, about twenty acres to a shot, and they're all prosperous little farms, at that; which gives you an idea what the land will do. Then there's another class of farmers—about fifty altogether, and among them they own the rest of the two hundred thousand acres. You figure that out for yourself. Fifty into two hundred thousand is four thousand acres apiece!" As he said this he covered his eyes with his hand and shook his head sadly. "Four thousand acres breaking their hearts growing stuff for you while you sit back and curse the foreman for not doubling the profits so you can have two yachts instead of one!"

A sort of horror fell upon the face of the consul. He went on: "But that's not all, dear friend. Tarry a while. Of the fifty, forty of 'em have a hundred thousand of the acreage. The other hundred thousand are divided among ten grand moguls, ten little princelets with ten thousand acres apiece."

"What do they raise on this land?" asked Jerry.

"Anything they think of planting—coffee, sugar, tobacco. The only things they don't grow are the things they've forgotten to plant. Those ten little kings own the rest of the island. They work together in a clique. They control the forty because they control not only the market but the social affairs of the island, and through controlling the forty they control everything. Suppose I should offend one of the ten? In twenty-four hours wheels would begin to spin in Washington; twenty-four hours after that a nasty little note would be on its way to me—or maybe a cablegram."

"Speed burners, eh?" Jerry interjected.

"Money's no object, of course. By degrees they're eating up the forty smaller fellows, and they're edging out and taking in the little holdings of the five thousand. Give them a few more years and they'll have the whole island under their thumbs."

"And the fifty are the poker trees?" Jerry asked, leaning back in his chair and caressing his lean fingers, never thickened by harder labor than the swinging of a quirt.

"With fences," the consul added, and he looked at Jerry with attention.

"I wonder," said Jerry, "if you know the names of the fifty?"

"I might be able to get a list," the consul replied without enthusiasm. He drummed his fat fingertips against the top of the table. "In a way," he continued, "anyone who acted as a sign post and pointed me on in my journey would have to be considered in. Peyton, I see that you are a fellow of intelligence. This is a devil of a job, and I don't get many asides."

The cowpuncher waved his hand.

"Frankly," the consul continued, "have you enough money to put up a front that will carry you through the fences?"

The fingers of Jerry wandered beneath his coat and touched the butt of his forty-five. "Between you and me," he said, "the best thing I have is a friend who'll back me for all that's in him."

"He'll plunge with you?"

"To the limit."

"He's a strong one?"

"I've never been able to faze him," said Jerry.

The consul drew out a fountain pen and an envelope and began to write on the back of it.

"Names?" said Jerry. "Trees," said the consul.

"Suppose you begin with the top of the gang and

work down—just offhand; I like to pick things by the sound of 'em."

"Sure. Well, there's the De Remi family. Old French crowd and the cream of social doings in the island. Then I suppose you could bunch in order the Franklins, the Ramseys, the Parkhursts, the Van Huytens, and the Da Costas. They're all old stuff in St. Hilaire. There's a newer set, too, that figures in with the old gang; the Quests, the Gentreys, the Langleys, and the Pattraisons. That's the list of the upper ten. They're the Four Hundred of this joint, plus the guardian angels, and the ruling hand. They're the ones I have to kowtow to"—his face darkened—"and they're the ones who pat me on the back and send along the good word—when they think to do it. I make myself handy for them—sort of errand boy, you know, between them and Washington— and now and then they ask me up to tea and tell me to drop in any time. You know?"

Jerry had never been to a tea, but he had learned, among other things in his brief and rather crowded life, that most valuable of all conversational assets, the ability to use a timely silence. He said not a word, and the consul felt that he was wholly comprehended.

"Suppose you begin at the bottom of the list," said Jerry. "This Pattraison outfit?"

"They and the Quests and the Gentreys and the Langleys," said the author, "are a new fry on the island. Of course they're big guns compared with the small landowners, but, after all, the Pattraisons aren't the last word. You know? Old Henry Pattraison is a card. He was a brewer, they say, before he sank a big wallop of an investment in St. Hilaire; there's a sort of custom here of forgetting the past of a family and judging it purely by its St. Hilaire record, but a brewer was a bit strong even for St. Hilaire's customs. They frowned him down, for a while; but after a while they forgot about his past and remembered that he had one of the best estates in the island and that eventually his heirs would be among the social leaders. Couldn't keep 'em from it. So they took in Mr. Pattraison. Also, he's a hearty old soul, clean as a whistle and game to the core."

"That sounds all right to me," said Jerry. "Now the Langleys."

"I put them down in the lower flight because they're newcomers like the Pattraisons," the consul went on. "As a matter of fact, Langley himself was in bad odor for a time. As I said before, people are judged by what they do in St. Hilaire, not by what they did before. Nobody knew what Langley was before he came here, but he pulled a bad one before he'd been long in the island. He got a small holding in the hills—all the central part of St. Hilaire is hilly, you know—and then before the people knew it he had grabbed almost all of Guzman's property, and today old Don Manuel has just a clump of trees and a smile to live on. It's a long story—the one they tell about the way Langley cut in on Don Manuel Guzman. Anyway, he got the land, and the De Remi crowd wouldn't receive him for a long time afterward.

"Then Patricia came out. You know the way a girl does? One year she's a skinny kid, mostly legs and elbows; the next time you see her she's in blossom and knocks your eye out with a full-grown woman's smile. Well, Patricia bloomed like that and she's an extra fine flower. St. Hilaire took one look at her and then fell all over itself being nice to the whole family. James Langley wasn't overwhelmed. Not by a long distance. He's a frosty sort of chap, anyway; never speak to him but I come within an ace of calling him Sir James, you see? Well, he saw that Patricia was the biggest social power in St. Hilaire. He had the young men of the island in the palm of his hand. No matter what their parents wanted to do, their sons were sure to break away and come to the girl—and she's a beauty, man! So Langley sat back and watched and let the first lot of 'em bark their knuckles against his doors without opening to them. Finally he let them in one by one, and he let them in in such a manner that today he's the social dictator of St. Hilaire. I suppose old Mrs. De Remi—Madame, they call her—runs him close when it comes to a pinch, but, all in all, Langley is the king. Mrs. Langley isn't a forward sort; but her husband has the big ace in Patricia and she can be played every day. Nobody has a successful party unless she's there; nobody thinks the landscape is complete unless her face is in the offing. You see? The De Remi crowd itself is helpless against a girl like that. They may regain part of their prestige after she's married, but if her father uses his head and marries her off to one of the first-flight families, he'll still be the dictator."

"It looks as if the Langley crowd would be a good one to get by the heel," said Jerry carelessly.

"They would well enough, but look sharp there. Langley is a fox. And there's only one word in that house—James Langley!"

"To the devil with him, then," Jerry said coldly. "Let's go on to the next best bet."

15

Before night, Jerry had a map of the island; before he went to bed he had studied out all the main features, and, above all, he knew every approach to the house of James P. Langley. His plan, like the plans of most intelligent men, was eminently simple. He would go straight over the hills, enter the plantation of James Langley, shoot his man, and come straight back to the harbor. There he would hire one of the big launches which he had seen gliding about the harbor and go for the mainland—or for one of the larger islands to the east where there was room for an able-bodied man to hide. With all this arranged in his mind, he undressed, bathed, and retired for a perfectly sound sleep.

In the morning he was awakened by a light weight striking his chest. He sat up and saw a bright colored bird sitting on the foot of the bed, looking at him without alarm. It was only a sugar bird, on its eternal quest for insects, but Jerry could not know this, and to him there was something preternatural in the wisdom of the little head tucked to one side and the eyes that glittered at him without fear.

"If you've come to advise me, partner," said Jerry to the bird, "fire away."

The bird flew to the window sill and looked back at him. "If it's action you want," said Jerry, getting out of bed, "I'm all set." And when the bird at once darted through the window into the open air outside, a thrill went through Jerry. He felt that the omen was good, and at once he began to sing.

He was singing again when he left the little, shabby hotel after a breakfast of strange fruits and abominable coffee, and hired a horse for the day. That a man should go with music in his heart to kill another may appear unforgivably callous; but, in Jerry's code, it was established so firmly that an insult to his dead father must be avenged with death, that to shrink from it would have been to him what a denial of God is to most men. He accepted a stern necessity; and though the horse was saddled with a pad which was a novel form of equitation to the cowpuncher, and though the revolver irked him beneath the waistband of his trousers, yet he sang as he rode because he was nearing the end of his quest.

Jerry was so happy now that he noted only the fine road before him, and the glossy brilliance of the tropical foliage on either side of him. Sometimes the sun set a whole field of it flashing so that he was almost blinded, but aside from such times, or when a strange new scent struck him, Jerry paid as little heed to the country through which he rode as if it had been the old familiar way from the ranch to Sloan.

So he came to a great stone fence that ran out of sight on either side, and straight before him was the end of the road, blocked by an iron gate of towering size. On a pillar beside the gate these words were deeply carved in the stone: "Langley Manor." It struck Jerry with a sense of fatal significance that the end of his trail should be the end of a road as well.

A black boy came out and opened the gate unquestioningly to the visitor; Jerry tossed him a quarter and went through onto a winding gravel way which wove from side to side, fenced with enormous palm trees. Then he saw before him a house with a mighty façade, and twelve pillars of bright stone going up the height of two stories, in the center, about the portico. There were other columns, on the wing entrance. That was where vehicles drove up, he saw.

For a single instant Jerry wondered if he had not come all this distance on a wild-goose chase—for how could the owner of this great estate possibly be the holdup artist who had taken his father's gun in malice, some three months before?

Imagination rarely took a violent hold upon Jerry's mind, however. Presently he gave his horse to another black boy—there seemed a limitless stock of them moving about—and spoke to a formidable porter at the front door—a white man, who felt the dignity of his position. He made way immediately for Jerry and took his hat. Then he asked for the name.

"Tell Mr. Langley," said Jerry, "that I wish to surprise him. When he sees me he'll understand why I don't want to be announced." He continued, smiling broadly upon the other: "Don't even describe me to him." Then, chuckling openly: "In fact, it would spoil the whole business if you tell him what I look like!"

The guardian of the door bowed, as one who disdained such boyishness, and having conducted the visitor through the door into the largest room Jerry had ever seen, he disappeared. The cowpuncher made sure that he was alone in the room—it required a full moment to sweep the big floor space and be certain—and then he stepped to the curtain through which the servant had gone. Behind the edge of it he saw the other going unhurriedly up the stairs. And such stairs! They wound out of the level of the reception hall with the dignity of a swerving river. They invited one's eye up, slowly, and when the glance had traveled for a distance up the stairway, it was easier to look up to the ceiling of the reception hall and appreciate the loftiness of that apartment.

As for the room in which he then stood, Jerry now looked about him only long enough to locate a hidden place from which he could command the doorway unseen. There were three which answered the purpose nicely. He chose a great tapestry which a draft from the open window was already furling back at one side. Here he could stand and see everything that passed through the door; yet he would be perfectly concealed. He would call out the name of Langley as soon as the latter entered, step out as he did so, and when the master of the house turned he would give him time to go for his gun first. So much Jerry decided as he stood behind the tapestry. Then he began to listen to the silence of the house.

It was so intense that a foolish fancy came to him that his approach had been noted, the servants and the master warned, and now by scores they were softly creeping up to surround the room in which he stood. Yet, a moment later, he realized that it was only the size of the place and the thickness of the walls that cut off the sounds of kitchen life and housecleaning activities which to Jerry were inseparable from the conception of such a dwelling.

He thought now of the immense importance of the life which he was about to end. It was the power which had built the wall against which he leaned; it was the hand which hung the tapestry before him; it was the will that ordered this very silence. If that life were taken the whole fabric would crumble. That big domestic who had gone with such leisurely dignity up the stairs, how he would leap as he heard the shot which killed James Langley! What uproar would rush into this room; and after that, a quiet, with only one or two women near the dead body—

Such thoughts as these unnerve a man. Jerry stopped himself and reversed the direction of his mind. He recalled again how he had pleaded with the robber not to take the Voice of La Paloma; he again saw Hank Peyton making the weapon a death gift to him. And just as his mind had reached that flinty hardness, there was a soft step. He looked, and saw a middle-aged man with black hair and a pair of shiny black eyes standing in the door of the apartment, looking about with a frown of bewilderment. Beyond a shadow of a doubt this was the man. He raised a hand to his thick mustache, and the hand was of womanish slenderness and pallor.

"Langley!" called Jerry, and slipped out from behind the tapestry.

His own hand was hanging in midair, ready for the lightning reach of his gun; but the master of the house turned without haste and faced him.

"Get out your gun," said Jerry, keeping his voice soft. "I'm here for you!"

The hand of the other stirred, and Jerry's leaped to the butt of his weapon—and then he saw the hand keep on rising until it was stroking the square, rather fat chin.

"He'll deny that he knows me," said Jerry to himself.

At that moment the master of the house remarked: "So it took you three months to get here, eh?"

"Look," said Jerry, and he glided a step closer, "I'm giving you a square break. You've got a gun on you. Get it out. You can make your move first; I'll allow you that much."

"Tut, tut," the other replied. "Three months of travel and still hot for more roadwork. My dear boy, you're a perfect demon when it comes to energy."

"I'll count three," said Jerry. "I know you've got a gun, and I'm going to make you use it. When I say 'three,' if you don't draw, I'm going to shoot you. You've got nothing else coming to you."

16

He counted slowly, and the white hand merely moved from the chin to the mustache. The bluff did not work. It did not even begin to work.

"No one looking on at this scene," Langley said, "would ever be able to believe that you're the son of old Hank Peyton. I'll tell you what, Jerry, men aren't what they used to be. You haven't the nerve to shoot a man in cold blood."

Jerry had seen many cool men in his day—he was fairly cool-headed himself—but he looked on Langley now, as he might on a superhuman creature.

"We'll go into the little room behind you," said Langley. He came to the door and waved Jerry in ahead of him.

"Thanks," said Jerry. "You go first."

The host smiled and went straight to a chair. "Sit down," he said, waving to another.

"I'm easier standing," said Jerry.

"Yes, it does make it clumsy to get out a gun—sitting down—unless you know the trick," he added tauntingly.

Jerry flushed and, accepting the challenge, he drew up the chair squarely before Langley, and with its back to the wall. He sat down on the very edge of it.

"Very well done," said the other approvingly. "I won't offer you a smoke, however," he added, "because I always feel that smoking with a man is like eating at his table. It's rather hard to treat him as an enemy afterward."

Jerry watched, and his eye was as sharp and steady as flint. "Get into your talk," he said. "Get on with it. But if you've touched a button or anything like that, if you've sent a high sign for some of your servants to come flocking around me, remember that I'll get you before they can get me, my friend!"

The host tipped back his head and laughed and laughed and laughed. Jerry watched, fascinated, as the fat throat puffed and shook.

"Dear me," James P. Langley said, as his merriment subsided, "I almost like you for that, my boy. You've been reading quite a bit of trash, I see. Buttons to press and trapdoors, too, eh? Come, come, you're too old for that."

"All right," Jerry said, leaning suddenly back and smiling in turn at the other. "I'm not in a rush. If this is the game, I'll play it this way."

"Oh, I don't put you down for a fool," Langley replied at once. "You've done two things very well. First, my trail was a hard one to follow. I suppose it was the gambler in Chambers City that tipped you off?"

Jerry shrugged his shoulders.

"You don't need to be reticent on his behalf," said the other, and the well-trimmed mustache bristled a disagreeable trifle. "I know that's the only place you could have learned what you wanted to know. You got him to talk, eh?"

"Also, I won quite a stake from him," and Jerry smiled.

"That's item number two for you, then," said Langley. "The third thing is that you're right about the gun. I have a revolver with me. I always have, in fact."

"And you just sit here and let me browbeat you, eh?" said Jerry.

The host grew pale to the eyes.

"It's hard to stand abuse," he said. "But I'll have to."

The fighting devil in Jerry welled up into his eyes and ran back to his heart twice; a cold sweat was standing out all over his body, and he was shaking before that was over, but he had kept from drawing his gun.

"It's hard, isn't it?" the other remarked. "But I've known very few men in my life who could kill in cold blood. You think you can and your nerves are all set for it, but when it comes to meeting the other fellow's eyes you weaken, eh?"

Jerry sat very still and thought. Every ounce of mental strength in his brain went into the effort.

"Langley," he said, when he had finished the struggle, "I think you're not straight; I think you're a crook."

The other lighted a cigar and puffed at it, then held it posed as though he were listening to an entertaining story.

"I think you're a crook," said Jerry, "and a lot of little things along the road to St. Hilaire have just about convinced me of it. But there's one chance in ten that I'm wrong. I'm not reserving anything. You did a yellow thing back at Sloan. You got me when I was helpless and you took something from me. If you can explain that away, I'll get up and say good-by and never look at your ratty eyes again. That's square, I think. Now explain."

The older man squinted through a mist of smoke. He looked up to the ceiling and then down at the floor. "That's a square opening for me," he said. "But I can't take advantage of it. All I can say is this: The only big mistake I ever made in my life was in rating a very clever man as a fool. You see, I treated the man as a fool, and he took me off guard. Gad, it seems impossible that I could have done it, now that I look back. He twisted me around his finger. The result is, the clever man put me in such a position that I can't explain how I happened to take your father's gun. It's impossible. I could tell you a story, but then you'd ask questions, and your questions would blow up the tale."

He puffed again at the cigar thoughtfully.

Jerry raised his left hand and brushed it across his shining forehead without obscuring his sight. "One thing more," he said. "If you give me back the gun, I think I can call the game off now. I'll not try to think it out."

But still the host shook his head.

"I've just been thinking of that," he said, "but the clever man saw through even that chance. I can't give the gun back to you."

"Then," said Jerry, "as sure as the sun's going to rise I'm going to drill you, Langley."

"Tut, tut," said the other. "You've already had your chance and you've failed. I know your mind, lad. I've stepped into it. You can't pull a gun until the other fellow has made the first move. Now, if I were to go for my revolver, I'd get it out, and I'd get it out before you had yours halfway to the mark. I'd kill you, my son; but when you were dead what earthly good would it do me? None whatever; instead, it would do me a tremendous harm. You see, large things are built on small, and if I were to kill you, this entire house would topple about my ears."

That whiplash flicker of his eyes went up and down the body of Jerry Peyton and then burned into his face.

"Nothing would please me more," went on Langley, "than a moment alone with you out in the mountain desert—say somewhere near Sloan, where a community is not so shocked by manslaughter. Unfortunately, we are some three thousand miles and more from Sloan." He paused and sighed. "And we are on the island of St. Hilaire, where mankilling is looked upon not as a vocation, but as a sin. You've no idea what a great difference that makes. For instance, if you were to be irritated past the point of endurance—if, I say, you were to do the impossible and draw your gun and shoot me—a dozen telephone messages would be sent out instantly from this house, and then the messages would be repeated at the farther end, so that in five minutes the entire coastline of this island would be watched and guarded. Every boat would be inspected to make sure that you were not on it, and little launches with machine guns mounted on 'em would slide up and down the coast to see that you didn't drift to sea."

He had talked so long that the cigar had almost gone out, and he now prevented this evil by puffing rapidly; his head appeared, presently, through a dense cloud of smoke, the eyes glittering at Jerry.

"You see," went on Langley, "this might be called a cooperative system of society. Do you follow that?"

"I'm followin' you so close, partner," said the big man, and he stretched himself in his chair, "that I'm wearing calluses on your heels. Go on."

The host looked at him with singular respect and cold observance commingled; he was thinking of the long, powerful body of a great cat, stretching with sleepy eyes, but incredibly alert at the same time.

"In this cooperative system," continued Langley, "we all work together to make it uncomfortable for the criminal. We don't consign all our legal interests to the hands of one sheriff, as they do at Sloan. Instead, we all step in and catch the disagreeable member of society and exterminate him with no more compunction than one would step on a snake."

"Me being the snake," said Jerry and grinned.

He was met by a flash of white teeth.

"I'm glad you understood so well," Langley went on; "for you are here in the midst of a net. It might be said that you rest on the palm of the hand of society, and if you bite the skin which holds you, the fingers will close and crush you out of recognizable shape. On the other hand, suppose that I were to shoot you down. In that case the danger would not be nearly so great. I would be kept under surveillance, to be sure; but I could readily escape from actual physical danger. All the same, a vital blow would be struck at the foundation of my work and ambition. I have said that if I kill you this house will tumble about my ears, and I mean this almost literally. I am not a mild man in a crisis, and the people of St. Hilaire would not endure another outbreak on my part. I should find my social position destroyed, the prospects of my family irretrievably ruined, or, at the least, the work of many years blown away in one puff of wind."

He lowered his voice toward the close of this speech until it became no louder than the murmur of a bee buzzing inside a room on a bright, still day. There was also the hidden anger in this murmur; it carried the hint of a sting.

"You're a bright man," Jerry said dryly. "You're too bright, almost. But you can't hold up. You can't stand the gaff. Suppose I pick a time when you have a lot of St. Hilaire's social knockouts around you; suppose I step up and call you hard, insult you in front of the gang. That'll make you go for your gun, eh?"

There was that same mirthless flash of white teeth, the same bristling of the precisely trimmed mustache.

"In many ways," said the rich man, "you are a child, Peyton. If you did that, I'd simply denounce you to the police as a madman and have you locked up."

"You'd be disgraced, though," said Jerry. "They'd see you're yellow."

"Not at all," said the other with meaning. "Whatever people may privately think of me in St. Hilaire, my courage, at least, has been placed beyond question. Come, my boy, look about you and see how complete the net is. I speak without passion and without fear of you; your position is impossible; therefore, look about you, admit the fact, and withdraw at once."

With one long, inward glance Jerry obeyed and saw that, as Langley had said, there was no escape. But being brought up against an impenetrable wall, his anger rose. It was a wall of words, after all; it was an obstacle created by the talk of this cool fellow with the glistening eyes.

In his helplessness Jerry let his glance rove. He then saw, close to him, a writing desk of ebony. It was one of those rare bits which are carved elaborately, and yet the minute carving is made subordinate to the line of the piece; the slender legs were yet strong enough and they rose from an adequate base; one would not be afraid to rest the weight of his elbow upon that desk. It was polished until, though it stood in the shadow, it glimmered, as though shining in the content of its own beauty. On the smooth surface lay a paper knife; it was silver, with a handle roughened by emeralds set into the metal, and on the surface of the dark ebony there was a reflection, a white streak for the silver and a green light for the emeralds—so that the knife seemed to be floating.

Upon these two things of beauty Jerry stared; for to him they reconstructed the whole fortune of the rich man and signified more than the rest of the house. The desk, carved like a jewel, the paper knife, a jewel indeed, left carelessly upon the surface of the desk— Jerry calculated absently that the entire value of the main street of Sloan would not duplicate that paper cutter. He looked up to Langley and sighed.

"It looks to me," he said, "as though you're right."

"Good," the millionaire said. It was a great mistake, that satisfied nod, for no man, and particularly no young man, likes to have his conclusions taken for granted. But Langley was victorious, he felt, and now he rushed on foolishly: "Of course, I'll see that all arrangements are made for your trip back, and it will be a pleasure to refund the money you have spent on this unfortunate excursion; in fact—"

"The devil!" said Jerry with infinite disgust. It made Langley open his eyes. "I said it looked to me as though you were right," said the big man, "but I'll be hanged if I'll go on the looks of it. I can't plug a man who won't pull a gun. You're right there. I can't make you fight by insultin' you in public. Well, there's still some other way I can hit you. I don't know how it is, but I'll find that way; and I'll make you come to me foamin', Mr. Langley; I'll make you come to me like a cow bawlin' for her calf; I'll make you come ravin' and beggin' for a chance to get a shot at me; I'll make you want to do murder, m' friend." He leaned a narrow, hard fist on the surface of the writing desk. "As a matter of fact, Mr. Langley, I don't think that's anything new to you!"

So saying, he straightened, and backed with long, light steps through the door. Langley watched him, interested, and then noted the swiftness and ease of the sidewise leap which carried the Westerner out of sight behind the wall. There was an ominous grace about his actions that made Langley think, not for the first time, of some big, half-tamed panther, playing in his cage. But the bars against which Jerry Peyton spent himself were the bars of civilization.

While he thought of these things, Langley picked up the paper knife from the ebony desk and looked at it curiously. The hard fist of Jerry had rested upon it, and it was sadly bent; the jeweler would have to straighten it.

17

The stable boy before the house of the master had the reins jerked from his hands, and he had barely time to catch a silver coin that was flung to him while Peyton vaulted into the saddle. The boy was used to seeing expert riders mount, but something in the manner in which this stranger flung himself through the air and landed lightly in the saddle on a horse that stood a good sixteen hands and a half, made the boy gape; he remained gaping while Jerry jerked the horse from a standing start into a full gallop with a merciless twist of spurred heels; then horse and rider shot off down the road and the shadows of the palms were brushing across them.

It was not the road by which he had come to the house, and Jerry did not care. He went blindly at top speed until the rush of wind against his face had cooled his blood sufficiently for him to begin thinking.

In the old days, when he felt after this fashion, he used to jump into the saddle on the buckskin. She took part of the mad humor out of him with her bucking, as a rule, and he spent the rest of it hunting for trouble with the first man he met. Around Sloan men were astonishingly accommodating when it came to providing trouble; but in this infernal island—

He brought the horse to a stand with a wrench on the reins that almost broke the poor brute's jaw, for through the tree trunks just ahead of him he made out the flash and blue shimmer of the sea. It was everywhere about him, then. It was crowding into his back yard, in fact. He sent his trembling horse out onto the brow of the hill and looked down where the surf came boiling on the beach and then slid back to the deep places. It leaped in tricky currents, and he saw what had been a smooth place before suddenly involved in a deep whirl that sucked the foam under and then threw it up again.

To Jerry water meant, on the whole, nothing more than the sleepy old Winton River, and he looked on the ocean with disgust. He remembered, too, the way the ship had ridden the waves, bucking until one's stomach commenced almost to float. So he hated this blue ocean and its green margin; above all he hated it because it drove back into his mind the memory that he was helpless—that he could never escape if he shot down Langley.

As if to complete his picture of isolation, as if purposely sent to drive him to a frenzy, a long, low-lying launch sneaked into view around the end of the promontory and glided across the bay. How could he escape from such a seagoing greyhound as that?

He found his horse shaking again; and then he

discovered that the animal was terrified because he had ridden so close to the edge of the hill, where the soil crumbled away and dropped in what was almost a cliff to the sea. At the sight of his horse's fear all the mad, sullen child boiled up in Jerry, all the hate that he felt for Langley and the sea and the fate which had sent him to this accursed island. He spurred the gelding until he stood straight up, with a groan, and then struck on all fours in full gallop. He strove to swerve inland, but the iron arm of Jerry wrenched his head over and made him race along the very verge of the cliffs.

Sometimes the ground gave way under his pounding hoofs. Sometimes his hindquarters sagged as a miniature landslide commenced and threatened to suck the horse over the brow of the hill, until the gelding was tortured into a hysteria of fear as strong and as blind as Jerry's hysteria of rage. He ran now where Jerry guided him. He went fearlessly along that crumbling cliff edge. He even strove to swerve and leap into the abyss when the yell of the cowpuncher rose and blew tingling behind him; but the man kept him true to his course, not a foot allowed on the danger side of it and not a foot allowed toward safety. He kept on until Jerry felt the forelegs pounding, felt the hindquarters sag, and knew that the gelding was almost spent.

All at once his own passion left him. He swung the gelding over to a firm little plateau and brought him to a down-headed halt. For a moment the panting of the horse lifted him slightly up and down in the saddle. He himself was panting, now that his rage had been converted into weariness; and when he slipped off the horse and remorsefully patted the flanks of the gelding, he would have given a great deal indeed if his prank had remained unplayed.

It was at this moment of depression that he looked over the croup of the horse suddenly, and saw an old man standing on the hilltop above him with folded arms, watching him solemnly. Indeed, his pose was one of almost affected dignity and reserve. He held his hat in his hand, so that it came under one elbow, and the wind was lifting the misty white hair, which he wore rather long for an ordinary man. He stood with one foot advanced in that position of self-control and balance which the world for some reason has connected with that nervous, active genius, Napoleon.

For the rest, there was no semblance at all between this man and the conqueror. He was of an attenuated leanness and very tall. Even from this distance Jerry could see that his head was small and his nose large. There was about him a sort of cruel dignity and scorn; it made Jerry think of a bald eagle surveying his kingdom of the air from a crag. He was almost surprised when he saw the old man shake his head in disapproval and became aware that this majestic figure was watching him. Because the other stood with head uncovered, Jerry instantly swept off his own hat and bowed.

Among the maxims of Hank Peyton, uttered when he was drunk, but observed whether drunk or sober, and impressed even upon Jerry's infancy with brutal force, was the following: "They's three things you got to sidestep and handle with a long rein: an old hoss, an old man, and a woman."

There was a little white scar which showed over Jerry's eye when he flushed; it marked an occasion when he was a very small boy and had spoken back to his mother. Hank Peyton had promptly knocked him down with the butt end of a loaded blacksnake. That lesson of courtesy was never forgotten by Jerry; and if he was ever tempted to forget, the scar reminded him. So he stood with his broad-brimmed hat in his hand and waited for the older man to address him.

As for the other, he stood for a moment surveying Jerry, and finally came down from the hilltop with a long, sure step, surprising in so old a man, and as dignified as his standing appearance.

"Good morning," he said. "I am Manuel Guzman."

"Sir," said Jerry, "I'm glad to know you. My name is Jeremiah Peyton, and I hope I haven't been riding over your land."

A cloud came on the brow of the old man, and Jerry remembered what he had heard from the consul.

"When you passed that point," said Don Manuel, "you entered my estate."

"I'm sorry," said Jerry.

The old man was silent; and a sense of guilt came to Jerry. He felt as if he had been spied upon and a weakness observed.

"I am sorry for your horse," the other replied calmly. "You are a wild rider, Señor Peyton."

Rebuffs were bitter food for Jerry. He had to waste a frown on the ground before he could look up and meet the eye of Don Manuel calmly. Then he was surprised to see a smile gradually spread over the lean face.

"For my part," said the Spaniard, "I keep away from my horses when I am angry. Or perhaps it was the horse itself that angered you?"

"The hoss is a fool hoss," said Jerry gloomily. "Look at him! Winded already, and his spirit about busted."

"By a ride on the edge of a cliff," said the old man, smiling more broadly. He looked narrowly at Jerry. "I thought you were going into the sea when you rounded that point."

Jerry looked back. The point was marked by a great boulder of red stone, and between the boulder and the sea drop there was only a meager footpath. Jerry shuddered.

"Did I ride around that rock?" he asked.

The old man was silent again and appeared to be thinking of other things.

"You must come up to my house with me," he said, "and sit down for a time. Your nerves are upset. I have some whiskey you shall taste, if you will."

"Lead the way," Jerry said instantly. "I'm so dry"—he paused to find a sufficient word—"that my throat crackles every time I draw a breath."

The Spaniard chuckled and led the way over the hilltop from which he had just descended. It gave an unexpected view of a low, broad valley, covered with a thick green crop on this side, and where it went up toward a range of hills beyond Jerry could see the regular avenues of an orchard. "Once," the Spaniard said, pointing, "that land to the hills was in my estate. However, I have still land enough. Follow me, sir."

He took Jerry down the slope and up again, until they reached a plateau densely covered by a growth of gigantic palms and trees almost as tall. In the center of this little forest there was an opening, where they found the house. It was built solidly of sawn rock, a single story sprawling around a patio with the usual fountain in the center. There was an arcade about the patio, and the stone floor, newly washed, was unbelievably cool to the eye. It was a green rock, worn deeply in places.

Here they sat down in the shade, facing each other

across a little table. The chairs were never meant for comfort; at least, though the rigid backs may have fitted the form of the don, the larger body of Jerry overflowed them. He forgot the chair, however, when a barefooted houseboy in white cotton jacket and trousers came pattering out with a tray, and the whiskey and ice and seltzer were arranged between them.

"Are you staying long in St. Hilaire?" Don Manuel asked.

"You put me down for a newcomer, eh?" Jerry replied.

"No old inhabitant rides as hard as that," said the Spaniard, "at ten o'clock in the morning. In the morning and the evening—oh, they are reckless enough; but at ten o'clock the day begins to fall into a sleepy time and everyone yawns and drowses."

"Then," Jerry added, "you make an exception, señor?"

"With me it is different," said the old man. "I carry whip and spur within me; and in a way, sir, you might say that I also gallop along the edge of a cliff." He sighed. "To your happiness, señor."

Jerry bowed, and they drank together.

There is a period after liquor has passed the lips of two men when they sit and look at each other and can read minds. This brief moment stole over the old man and the young, and they sat regarding each other solemnly. The white-clad houseboy had brought a basket of fruit and knives, but Jerry refused it.

"I don't know how long I shall stay," said Jerry, reverting to the last question. "As soon as my business is over, I leave."

The Spaniard smiled again in his wise way. "And yet, señor," he said, "when I saw you careering along the hills, between the sea and the sky, one might say, I made up my mind that you were a prisoner in St. Hilaire."

"A prisoner?" repeated Jerry slowly.

"To your interests here," replied the Spaniard coolly. "A prisoner rebelling, however, against his captivity. I can remember a day," he went on, "when I rode very much as you rode along the hills, and I cared very little whether my horse fell into the sea or remained on the dry land."

He pushed the whiskey bottle toward Jerry as he spoke, but the latter sat, turning the bottle slowly.

"I can almost tell you why you rode that day," said Jerry.

"Señor?" queried the old man.

"You had spoken to Langley, eh?" said Jerry.

He saw the other quiver under the shock.

"Because," went on Jerry hastily, "I've just finished talking to the same fellow."

Don Manuel had raised the glass toward his lips, but now he lowered it again, untasted. An inspiration came to Jerry. He filled his own glass and poised it.

"I think," he said, "that there is a real reason for us to drink together. Once more, to your good health, señor."

Don Manuel looked long and earnestly at the American.

"I drink," said he, "to the kind fortune which has sent me a man."

18

The casual visit of the morning was extended until noon, and when the noon meal passed, there was a lazy warmth in the air which forbade travel.

When the evening approached, the don showed Jerry through the house, and, stopping in a room where the windows overlooked the sea, he said: "This is your place, sir, until you leave St. Hilaire."

It was impossible to refuse hospitality offered in this manner. Jerry made up his mind to formulate his refusal later on; but then came the dinner; and after they had dined, the night dropped about them and Jerry began to talk. The words flowed almost without his knowledge, and before he knew it he had laid his heart bare to Señor Guzman; he had told of the first meeting; he had told of the pursuit; he had told of the scene in Langley's study, and finally of his unquenchable determination.

They were sitting in the patio, and after the story was done, the Spaniard remained silent for a pause of embarrassing length, looking up at the stars. Finally he went into the house and returned with a candle. He placed it at the other end of the long court, so that the flame was merely a slender eye of light, tilted sidewise with its halo by the steady pressure of the northeast trades, which blow day and night unceasingly over St. Hilaire.

Don Manuel came and stood behind the chair of Jerry; the young man turned and looked up, but, with his hands on the muscular shoulders of the American, Don Manuel said, preventing him from rising: "There is a tale going the rounds," he said, "that at ten paces Señor Langley can snuff a burning candle; yonder candle, now, is about twice that distance, I think."

"Ah?" said Jerry, and as he spoke, he whirled in the chair.

He did not rise, but the gun leaped out of his clothes and exploded. The flame of the candle jumped and went out.

"Confound it!" Jerry said at the end of a moment of silence. "Too low or I would have trimmed it."

But the Spaniard went down and picked up the candle and came back carrying it in both hands. He stood, then, peering down at Jerry as though the candle still burned, and by its light he studied the stranger.

"I am out of practice," said Jerry, flushing, "but with my gun in shape and a bit of work to—"

Don Manuel raised a compelling hand and went into the house. When he came out again he said, without prologue: "It is because you have no way to touch the man's nerve, is it not?"

"How can I touch him?" Jerry replied sadly. "Can I

get at his property? Can I threaten him in any way? If he had a son, I might manhandle him; but I can't hit a man forty-five years old."

An air from an opera which had been popular twenty years before Jerry was born came whistling from the lips of Don Manuel. He sat with his chin in his hand. At length the music stopped short.

"Go to bed and sleep, my son," he said finally; "for you must get up with me at dawn, and then I shall show you the key to Señor Langley's heart."

"We're going to his house?" asked Jerry sharply.

"You must trust me," said the old man with a marvelously evil smile. The bitterness of half a life was summed up and expressed by that smile. "Be prepared, for in the morning you shall see the key to his heart."

From the first meeting it had seemed to Jerry that he sensed a base of rock in the nature of the Spaniard; and now he knew that misfortune had not taught him or bowed him. He was as rigid as he has been in the pride of youth, and in the place of the warm blood of the young man, his veins were filled with acid hate. Yet evil is usually more imposing than good; Jerry saw, when he lay in bed looking into the dark, that the only reason he had spoken to the Spaniard and told the whole story was because he recognized subconsciously the unholy fire in Don Manuel. He trusted to that fire now, and in this trust he fell into a profound slumber.

Once, it was a dreamlike thought, he seemed to part his eyelids slightly and look up at the form of the Spaniard in a robe of white, shielding a candle so that little of its light touched the face of the sleeper, but a bright radiance fell on Don Manuel. Jerry shuddered in his sleep.

When he next wakened, the hand of Señor Guzman was on his shoulder.

"Get up," said the host. "Here is a bathing suit which will fit you. You must be thoroughly awakened, so plunge into the tub of cold water that waits for you. When that is done, put on the bathing suit and come into the patio."

It was impossible to deny those eyes, so bright under their wrinkled lids; and before Jerry was fully awake he had gone through the routine which the host prescribed and stood beside him in the patio.

Don Manuel looked over his guest with an almost painful attention—as a trainer, say, looks over the trim muscles of an athlete—then he nodded as one who knew men. "Come," he said simply, and led the way from the house and over a terrace of grass to a hilltop which overlooked the sea.

The sun had not risen. To the east, over a gray mist along the horizon, the tints of the dawn were rolling up the sky; and one cloud, high above the rest, was burning with red fire. It sent a stain of crimson across the sea toward the two on the cliff.

"Well?" said Jerry.

"Are you cold?" said the Spaniard. He himself was wrapped in a heavy cloak.

"No," said Jerry Peyton. Indeed, the air was as mild as a spring noontide.

"Look down to the beach."

It was a drop of a hundred feet, at least; a long, white stretch of sand lay before him, and along its margin the waves rolled, broke into sudden lines of white, and then slipped swiftly up the shore.

"What's next? I see the beach."

"Patience."

It was odd to see the old man assume command. He paid not the slightest heed to Jerry, but began to walk up and down. The northeast wind sent his cloak flapping every time he turned to the end of his pacing. For the rest, he seemed to be looking up into the eye of this wind more than anywhere else, and a ghostly feeling came to Jerry that the Spaniard was about to receive a message out of the empty air. He, also, began to scan the horizon, and he started when Don Manuel stopped in his pacing and pointed suddenly down at the beach.

"The key to Señor Langley," said he.

And Jerry, looking down, saw a girl galloping a horse along the beach. She wore a light cloak, which blew behind her, and a scarlet cap covered her head. The blue cloak, the red cap, the cream-colored horse—she was sweeping along the beach like a bright cloud out of the sunrise. A clawlike hand caught the shoulder of Jerry and dragged him down behind a rock.

"She mustn't see you with me," said the Spaniard. "Not now."

"Is this part of the job you plan on, partner?" said Jerry coldly. "Spyin' on a girl?"

The cream-colored horse stopped, and the girl, dismounting, threw away the cloak, slipped the shoes from her feet, and ran down the beach toward the sea.

Jerry sat up, and when the Spaniard turned to him, he found that the boy's face was scarlet, and a white line showed above his eye.

"Did you get me up before sunrise," said Jerry fiercely, "to spy on a girl?"

The Spaniard blinked and then smiled.

In spite of the lessons of his father, in spite of the scar on his face, in spite of that fine Western scorn of anything connected with duplicity where women are concerned, Jerry looked again. It had been merely a causeless shock, he decided, as he watched her run along the beach in her gay bathing suit. As he looked, the water was struck to white about her feet, and then she dived under the surface. As the wave rolled swirling to the shore, the Spaniard smiled again at Jerry.

"That is the key to Señor Langley," he said. "That is his daughter, Patricia."

For a time Jerry stared at him stupidly. "Listen to me, partner," he said coldly, when he had finished his survey of that ancient, evil face. "I come from a place where bad men are pretty fairly thick, but bad men around women don't flourish in those parts. They wither away sudden. They get cut off at the root. You see?"

Don Manual made a slow gesture, with both the palms of his hands turned up.

"Señor Peyton," he said, "you are not wise. I point out to you a way in which you can make Señor Langley come to you as you wish, raving, with his gun in his hand, and you insult me for pointing out the way." He leaned over and laid a bony hand on Jerry's arm.

"Do not say it," Jerry murmured, the flush gradually leaving his face.

"That is much better, my son," said the Spaniard. "Now hear me calmly. You will go down to the beach. You will swim. When you come on shore you will be close to Señorita Langley. She will speak to you; you will speak to her. You will tell her your name. She will tell you her name. Is there any harm in that?"

"It looks straight to me," said Jerry cautiously. "What's it lead to?"

"To much," said Don Manuel. "It leads to everything

we wish. She will go home and remember you. You will be easy for her to remember."

"Me?" said Jerry, wide-eyed.

"Peyton is a simple name," said the Spaniard hurriedly.

"That's straight enough," murmured Jerry.

"And when she goes home she will tell her father that she has met you. Now, the Señor Langley is a stern man in his home. His word is law. Ever since she has become a young woman, the girl is used to hearing her father say, 'Receive this man,' and she receives him, or, 'Do not smile on this man,' and she makes her face a blank before him. There is always a reason. Such a man is too poor, too rich, or one is of the good blood and another is not. There is always a reason, and the girl obeys, for her heart has not been touched. Do you understand?"

"I partly follow you," said Jerry, frowning with the effort.

"A woman is like a blossom," the old man continued, watching the eyes of the American. "For a time she is hulled in green. And after that the green opens and she is stiff petals—a bud. But then, all on a day, a bee touches the bud, or the wings of a moth dust across it, or a leaf falls on it, and then it opens in that one day and lets the sun come into its heart. It is all in a day; and all in a day a girl steps into womanhood. Is that clear, señor?"

"I see something in it," admitted Jerry cautiously.

"But the Señor Langley does not see it," said Don Manuel. "He is the cold Northern race; his heart is ice; he cannot see the heart of a woman. But I am a Guzman, and I know. Old men and poets know women, my son, and I am a very old man."

"Go on," Jerry commanded sternly, as the Don paused.

"We return, then, to the moment when Langley

orders her to see this stranger she has met on the beach no more. He gives her a reason—she is not to make friends with every nobody she meets. Pardon me, señor."

"That's all right," said Jerry heartily. "I can see the old boy's face as he says it. Go on."

"She understands that this must be so; yet she is thoughtful, for when she mentions your name she sees her father start. It is a little thing—a lifting of the eyebrows. You see? But the girl sees it; she says, 'My father knows this man before.' So she asks her father to inquire about you and find out your past. Perhaps he does it; perhaps he tells her a lie. He dare not tell her the truth, and if he tells her a lie, who will know it is not the truth?"

"Wait a minute," said Jerry. "You don't know this Langley. She'll never guess it's a lie."

"I am an old man, and I know women," persisted Don Manuel stubbornly. "She will know it is a lie, and, also, she has the blood of her father in her and she understands. So she sits in her room and thinks. For one, two mornings she goes to another beach; but there is no good beach in St. Hilaire but my beach. She cuts her feet on the coral; she wades up to the ankles in slime and mud; and she thinks of the hard, clean, smooth sand of the beach of Don Manuel. It will be so!" He paused. "Also, she may remember you; you are different from the others, my son. So on the third morning she says to herself: 'What harm in going there? My father need not know. The man is not a viper.' So she comes on the third morning to the beach of Don Manuel."

"I follow all this," said Jerry. "Nobody likes to swim on a muddy bottom."

"You understand swimming, my son?"

Jerry thought of the place where the Winton drops into a wild series of cascades. Once he had gone down those rapids, swimming. "Yes, I swim a bit," he replied.

The Spaniard nodded. "That is still better. So she comes back, remembering how you swim."

"But what the devil does that lead to?"

"Everything. The apple of discord is thrown into the family of Don James! And the girl has kept a thing from her father."

"I don't like it," said Jerry sullenly. "I—I don't like that idea."

"Wait! The apple of discord is thrown into the family. Now the girl sees you every morning; for every morning she swims to keep the blossom in her cheeks that all St. Hilaire wonders over. Ah, I know! Also, she is come to the time. It is not far distant." He nodded, and his little, evil eyes glittered into the distance. "She knows the bees which buzz in St. Hilaire. She keeps her petals closed. They are nothing to her. But she hears a new sound. It is a lean wasp, fierce, swift, silent, strange. She opens her heart to it!"

"Partner," said Jerry with concern, "this early mornin' air must be going to your head. What the dickens are you talking about?"

"You shall see. The day comes when the girl goes to her father again and speaks of you. Then he has been disobeyed, and the madness comes over him. Have you seen him in his madness?"

"No."

"Ah, ah," murmured the Spaniard, "you have much to learn of Don James. Well, you will see it. But now go down to the beach. Go down my son."

"And in the end?"

"In the end he will know that he has been disobeyed.

He will seize his fastest horse and rush to my house. There, I trust, you will not be hard to find."

"Partner," said Jerry, "I begin to get your drift. He'll come ravin'—he'll come for the showdown?"

"He will come and shine like a flame—like a flame of a candle in my patio, señor."

But Jerry Peyton was already on his feet and going down the sandy slope of the hill toward the beach.

Don Manuel kneeled and pressed his face close to the rocks as he saw the lithe, muscular figure break from a walk to a jogging trot, and from a trot, as a sudden feeling of exultation came over him, into a full racing gait. A rock rose in his path. He hurdled it with a great leap and went on, his bare feet spurring the sand into little jets behind him. The old man clutched both hands to his heart.

"God give me grace!" he whispered. "Let her see him now."

His prayer was answered. She rose from the sea, shaking the water out of her face, at the same time that Jerry struck the shore. Two strides brought him up to the knees; he shot through the air, disappeared under the heaving front of a wave.

Don Manuel rose and walked stolidly toward his house.

"It is enough," he said; "she has now seen a man."

19

As for Jerry Peyton, the slope of the hill face had given such impetus to him that he forgot the girl, he forgot the scheme, he lost himself in the joy of speed, and when he slipped under the wave he came up with a long, powerful overhand stroke that shot him through the water. He had never swum in salt water before, and his swimming muscles, hardened to the work of fresh rivers and lakes, now whipped him along through the heavier, more buoyant, ocean. Also, it sent a tingle across his skin. He gave himself to his work. When a wave heaved up, trembling before him, he dived and came up in the calm water beyond. Past four lines of waves he swam, and then turned and made leisurely back for the land.

If it was pleasure to swim in the face of the sea, it was marvelous to have the big waves pick one up, unaware, and throw one bodily toward the land. He came with a crawl stroke now, rioting in the speed, and with foam about his shoulders; a mass of water lifted around him and tossed him up. When he came down, his knee struck sand.

He staggered up the beach, panting, and there he saw the girl, with one hand on her hip and dabbling one foot in the water. He came from a land where the girls have no fear of men, and yet he was unprepared for the directness of her eyes and the fearlessness of her smile. He was striding through the surf, tingling, his broad chest was working like a bellows, filling with that pure morning air, and then her glance stopped him.

"That last wave nearly tumbled you on your head, didn't it?" said the girl.

"Did it? I don't know. I was having too good a time to see. Never swam in the ocean before."

"You let them take you and float you," said the girl, "and you can ride them in—like a horse, almost."

He had stopped panting enough to look more closely at her now. He saw that her eyes were black, but they had not the glitter of her father's eyes. He was deeply grateful for that. He had an odd desire to step back so that he could throw her into a perspective and see her clearly—as if she were a mountain. He was surprised by the small, cold touch of awe; something that the Spaniard had said was true—something about flowers between the bud and the blossom.

"Show me how, will you?" said Jerry.

"Of course. Come on."

They went into the water side by side. "Who are you?" asked the girl.

"I'm Jeremiah Peyton."

"I'm Patricia Langley. Come on, here's a good wave!"

He was amazed by the ease with which she cut the water. Her round, active arms plied the water just ahead of him, and he held back to watch. She stopped in a rocking trough, treading the water. "How far out shall we go?"

"As far as you like," said Jerry.

"Oh, I don't care. I never get tired in the water."

"As far as you like," he repeated, treading water also.

"But there's the Long Reach," she said.

A wave obliterated them, but when he came up again he followed her gesture and saw a white streak out to sea. "What's the Long Reach?"

"I don't know exactly. Some kind of a crosscurrent or something like that. It forms from the mouth of the cove, several times a day, and then goes swirling out to sea. If you get caught in it, it's all day with you. Takes you miles and miles out. Billy de Remi was caught in it—poor Billy!"

The top of a wave spilled over her as she spoke. She came up laughing, and then struck out.

"You say when you want to turn back," she called back over her shoulder, and then the red cap was submerged as she struck out with a driving crawl stroke.

He could see that she was challenging his speed, and she slid through the water with remarkable rapidity; but a half a dozen strokes convinced Jerry that he could overhaul her when he chose. He drifted back, and then cut in around her and drew up on the side of the white line of water. Once or twice, as she turned her head for breath, her eye caught his and she flashed a smile at him; but on the whole she was strictly serious business.

She headed straight out to sea, and now Jerry could hear, louder than the noise of the surf behind them, the rushing of the white waters ahead of him. The girl also heard them, but she went straight on, lifting her head clear, now and then, to gauge the distance. An odd thought came to Jerry that she was testing him in this manner, and with a few hard strokes he pulled up even with her.

She came up, treading water, at that. She was white, but her eyes danced and she was smiling. "Shall we go on?"

"Just as you say," said Jerry, and smiled back.

She cast one gloomy look at him and immediately struck out again. Now the sound of the waters ahead filled Jerry's ears, but he kept even with her, and a little ahead, until an arm of boiling water reached out at them. They were swept far from their course and close together. Over the sound of the rushing he heard her cry; then she turned like an eel and hit out for the shore. It was a full minute of hard labor before she made headway. The current came foaming about her neck and made a wake behind her shoulders; once she turned her head and cried again at Jerry; but he, swimming with comparative ease close by, made no effort to aid her.

They were clear of the danger as suddenly as it had come upon them, and she brought her head up, treading water again.

"Why—" she began angrily.

"Well?" said Jerry, and grinned at her white face.

"It nearly got us!" panted the girl.

"I knew we were all right," he said. "You told me you knew these waters."

All at once she was laughing. "You're a queer one," she called, and headed back for the line of the surf.

He remembered, as he followed, that Don Manuel had said she would find him different. In fact, he was so full of many thoughts that he by no means grasped her lessons in surf riding. He saw a big wave take her and shoot her toward the shore, she riding lightly in the crest; and then the same wave caught Jerry, doubled him up, and rolled him over and over like a ball. He came up with sand in his ears, his nose, his mouth, and in his blindness staggered toward the waves again; but Patricia came, laughing, and led him up the beach. That misadventure seemed to restore her good humor. She was still laughing when he had washed himself clean again and turned on her.

"In my part of the country," Jerry said, "they don't treat a tenderfoot this way. Five minutes after I meet you, you take me within a yard of drowning, and then you roll me in the sand."

She was pulling on her shoes and lacing them. The instant before she had seemed more boy than girl; now she was wholly woman, and when she smiled up at him absentmindedly, he searched his mind for something to say, but his brain was a perfect blank. He looked around him—the sea, the hills, the wind, the sky, the sunrise rushed upon him, and he rejected them all. He wanted to say something, in fact, which would make her forget all those very things. A great gray bird flew in from the sea, and she raised her head slowly up and up, watching its flight—until he was conscious only of her parted lips, her eyes, and the line of her throat.

"I wonder what it is?" said Patricia, standing up and catching her cloak about her. The cream-colored horse came up to her; he was evidently a pet. "It's not a gull," said Patricia.

"Damn the bird," said Jerry with warmth. "I beg your pardon," he added hastily, as she glanced at him. "I wasn't thinking of what I said."

"I think you were," Patricia replied not altogether coldly. She surveyed him anew and liked him. "Wha in the world made you say that?"

"I don't know," said Jerry miserably. "I guess you're pretty peeved about it, eh?" He began to explain with a frown: "You see, I was about to say something when that bird flew over, and—"

"And then I interrupted you?" She observed him still again, for men did not usually tell her when she interrupted them. She had never seen a man who looked quite like that in a bathing suit. His face and neck were tanned and his hands were even darker to the wrist. But the rest of his body was as white as snow, and whenever he moved she could see long, unobtrusive, efficient-looking muscles at play. "What was it you were going to say?" she added.

"That's the point," and Jerry sighed. "You've made me forget it."

"You are queer," the girl commented, with a light laugh.

"I had an idea you'd think that," said Jerry gloomily.

"Why?"

"Because I feel mostly like a fool."

She had a wonderful resource of laughter, effortless and sweet to hear.

"Do that again," said Jerry.

"Do what?"

And he answered: "Laugh again; it's great to hear you.

She looked beyond him and saw that the sun was about to rise, her signal to depart for a beauty sleep before breakfast time; but she saw that he was enjoying her immensely, and, for some reason, it meant a good deal to see this fellow look at her with intense eyes; it seemed important, indeed, just to keep that big, power-ful body at play.

"I'm sorry that I made you forget that thing," said the girl.

"So'm I," Jerry replied unaffectedly.

"No idea what it was about?"

"It was about you."

"Oh!" murmured Patricia; she had been talked to so much by men that she was long past the stage when she glanced away or had to summon a flush when they talked personalities; instead, she was able to look direct-ly at them, and that always gave her a vast advantage. It always made the men feel that they were inane and that Patricia was formidably clever. But when she looked at Jerry he seemed too much absorbed in his own reflec-tions to note her. A surmise struck her that he had not consciously intended a compliment—that he was talking as naturally and as simply to her as he would talk to another man—that under the surface of those keen gray eyes and behind that rather homely face there was simply the heart of a boy. The moment she surmised these things something like a pang went through Patricia. She leaned against the side of the cream-colored horse and she watched Jerry with a wonderful, still look.

"It was about you," he was saying, "and it was impor-tant. I'll tell you," he continued, gathering head, "you're harder to talk to than most girls; do you know that?"

"No," said Patricia; she even forgot to smile, she was so intent studying him; and she was beginning to wonder why she usually was fencing with words when she talked to men—even the boys of the island, whom she had known ever since they were mere infants.

"Well, you are hard enough," said Jerry. "I never had

any trouble chatting with other girls. Nope, not a bit. Any old thing would do to start with."

"Oh!" said Patricia.

"But just now," went on Jerry, "I had an idea that you were about to get on your horse and go."

"I am," said Patricia, starting and gathering up the reins; but she did not turn toward the horse.

"I was afraid of that," said Jerry, "so I hunted around for something to talk about. I saw the ocean and the sky and the hills and the sunrise and all those things. You see?"

"Weren't they good enough to talk about?"

"If you're laughing at me, inside," Jerry said, "just do it right out loud. I don't mind. In fact, I like it!"

She did laugh at that; but not very long. "Go on," said Patricia. For she felt as if she were hearing a story. There was an element of suspense about everything he said.

"What I wanted wasn't any sea or sky stuff," said Jerry. "I wanted to say something about you."

"Oh!"

'Because," explained Jerry, "you seemed more important."

"Oh!" repeated the girl.

"Say," said Jerry, "d'you mind tellin' me what you mean by saying, 'Oh,' so much?"

"I don't know," murmured Patricia; then added hastily: "I mean, it seems to me that you started the conversation very nicely without that last remark."

"D'you think so?" said Jerry, and smiled with pleasure. "I'm no end glad of that. I'll tell you something," he said confidentially.

"What?"

"Oh, it isn't important. But I saw you go in swimming

from the top of that hill, and when I came down I was hoping that I'd be able to talk to you."

"When you came down the hill," said the girl thoughtfully, "were you trying to catch my eye?"

"As a matter of fact," confessed Jerry, "when I came down the hill my legs got to going so fast that I didn't think about anything but running. D'you ever try it? If it's steep, your legs get a funny feelin' around the knees."

"I'll try it, someday," and Patricia smiled. "I'm glad you did talk to me. How old are you?" she asked, apropos of nothing.

"I'm twenty-four," he said, as if it were the most natural question in the world. "How old are you?"

"You look more like eighteen or thirty-five, somehow," said Patricia, thinking aloud. And then: "What did I say?"

"That I looked sort of young," said Jerry. "I don't mind, because I'm growing older every day."

"You have a way of saying things," said the girl, "that makes me want to think them over. I'm still sorry about that lost remark."

"I can't remember what it was about," he answered, studying. "But I can tell you what I meant."

"All right." She kept continually breaking out with eagerness and then checking herself. Perhaps she felt from time to time that she was compromising her dignity.

"It was something to this effect: That it makes me happy to be here talkin' to you." He was looking down at the ground in his brown study as he said this, and she was glad that she did not have to answer. Also, it gave her a chance to look at his face without passing the barrier of his glance. "So happy," said Jerry, looking up quickly, "that I feel sort of grateful."

She put her foot in the stirrup and swung up.

"What's wrong?" asked Jerry, looking behind him.

"The sun," panted Patricia. "It's away up high."

"Isn't that natural for it to be there?"

"I have to go home. Mr. Peyton, why—"

"Yes? Stand still, fool hoss!" He caught the bridle close to the bit and took every tremor out of the horse with a twist of his fist. "Go on," said Jerry.

"Why don't you come to call?"

"At your house?" said Jerry.

"Of course."

"I'll tell you," and Jerry grinned. "If your dad ever saw me come through the door of your house, he'd start r'aring."

"Do you know dad?"

"Sure I do."

"Then you knew me all the time!"

"I never saw you before," Jerry replied with equal truth and evasion.

She admitted this with a nod, but now she was frowning as she looked at him; she was concentrating mightily on him. He had been interesting before, but if her father hated him, he must be important.

"What's dad got against you?"

"Ask him," said Jerry coldly.

"Something awful?"

"Ask him," repeated Jerry, and set his jaw. She found herself, in an instant, looking into an entirely different face, and it took her breath. Then that metallic light passed away from his eyes. It was a marvelous change.

"Perhaps—where—but where did you know him before?"

"Maybe he'll do the explaining," said Jerry calmly.

"Won't you even defend yourself?" cried Patricia.

"Defend myself?" Jerry said, and he smiled. "Why should I? Does your father do your thinkin' for you?"

"Of course not."

"Then you can make up your own mind about me out of what he says. I'll tell you this, though: He thinks I'm a cross between a fool and a rattlesnake."

"But—" said the girl. She stopped, with her lips parted, and it was easy to see that she was troubled.

"I won't keep you," Jerry said suddenly, and dropped his hand from the bridle. "Good-by."

She avoided his outstretched hand. "Why 'good-by'?" she said.

"Your dad won't let you see me again."

"I'm not a baby," said Patricia hotly.

Jerry smiled.

"What do you mean by smiling?" asked the girl.

He shrugged his shoulders, and suddenly she had slipped her hand into his.

"Adieu!" she called with a delightful accent, and went galloping down the beach.

He stood watching her for a long time; but when, as she reached the point of the beach, she looked back, he had turned and was striding up the hill.

"I wonder what he meant by that smile?" she repeated, and checked her horse to a hand gallop. It was easier to think at that pace.

20

He did not see Don Manuel until they came to the breakfast table together. The cloth was white and crisp, and against it there were some red-hearted melons so sweet and rich that one ate them with lemon. Jerry occupied himself strictly with business, and half of his melon was gone before Señor Guzman spoke.

"You had a long chat?"

"Yes," said Jerry.

There was not another interchange of words until breakfast was ended. The Spaniard employed every second of the silence to the full.

"Well," he said afterward, "she is delighted, no?"

"She?" echoed Jerry vaguely.

"No?" insisted the Spaniard.

"I don't know," Jerry replied.

"H-m-m," said Don Manuel. He added: "It is unfortunate that you don't like her."

"Who said I didn't like her?" Jerry exclaimed. "She's —lovely." He said after a moment: "And the daughter of Langley."

"Well," declared Don Manuel after a moment, "you are a strange fellow."

"Do I look strange?" asked Jerry.

"Ah, yes," said Don Manuel steadily.

"Well," said Jerry, "I'm sad as the dickens."

"Tush! That is too bad. What makes it?"

"I dunno." He looked wistfully at Don Manuel. "It's something like seasickness," said Jerry.

"The melon—yes," nodded the other.

"No," said Jerry, feeling for the place. "It's not my stomach. It's higher. It's an ache." He stood up. "It—it makes me feel as if I can't breathe in here!"

"We'll step out in the patio."

"Señor," called Jerry.

They were in the door; the tall old man looked down at Jerry, and his eyes burned deep in his head.

"Why did you send me down to see that girl?"

"To amuse you, my young friend."

"Don Manuel," said the American, "you're a clever devil."

"You are profane," Don Manuel remarked dryly, "and yet in a way you honor me."

"She asked me to call," Jerry went on. "I told her that her father would never let me in his house."

"What?" cried Don Manuel, and his bony hand dug into the arm of Jerry.

"I told her that he hated me, but she seemed to have an idea that her father might be wrong."

"Kismet!" whispered Señor Guzman, and snapped his fingers loudly.

"What's that?"

"You were inspired," said the Spaniard.

"She will never come again," Jerry replied and laid his hand against his throat.

"On the third morning," said Don Manuel. "And now, come. We will walk together."

They went again to that highest hilltop which overlooked all the valley and all the coast; sometimes, from beneath the screen of green and out of shadows, white spots showed in the sun, the laborers at work on the plantation. "My father, my grandfather, my great-grandfather," said Señor Guzman, "owned all this land as far as you can see; and I am the fourth in the line."

Jerry looked at him, and saw at what a price he retained his calm. "I'm sorry," said Jerry.

"For what?" asked Don Manuel.

"Because you lost it all."

"It shall be mine again," said Señor Guzman.

The American said nothing.

"It is that which keeps me alive," the Spaniard continued. "And the Lord sustains me to regain my heritage. I shall tell you. I am no longer a man; I am a ghost, with a purpose in place of life."

A chilly conviction came to Jerry that he had to do with a madman; that explained the fire in the eyes of the old man, if nothing else.

"It was long ago that I lay on my deathbed," said the Spaniard, "and while I lay dying, the Señor Langley came to me. He had loaned me money; he came to have the debt discharged, and he said that since I was ill he would not burden me with matters of this world.

"The priest waited even then to give me absolution.

The Señor Langley was thoughtful; he had only some papers which I must sign and then forget about all debts. I had strength to hold a pen and therefore I signed."

"Ah," said Jerry, and his voice rattled in his throat.

"But the good priest," continued the Spaniard, "had heard what Langley said to me. When he came in he warned me! I looked at my copies of the papers I had signed and saw that of all my estates I now owned only a tiny corner. A weight fell upon me; I lost my senses.

"When I awakened, they were making ready to prepare my body for burial, but I had slept and I had new strength. As I lay there, I knew that I had been spared to get my vengeance. And when after I had waited these many years, in quiet, I saw you, my son, I knew that He had put a weapon in my hand." He added: "The heat of the morning begins. Let us go into the house."

Over the valley a mist of the day's heat was beginning to rise. It thickened, and when Jerry looked back as they went through the trees, all the rich acres behind him and below were as mysteriously clouded as a reflection in a troubled water.

The next morning he went to the hilltop and sat on the rocks, waiting and watching; nothing came up the beach, and though he remained there until the heat burned his face, there was nothing to be seen but the glare of the sand and the shining water, and some gulls balancing in the northeast wind.

On the morning after that, he went again to the hilltop, but there was nothing to be seen, although he waited this time until his eyes ached from peering up and down the sand. He went back to the house, whistling.

"My son," said the Spaniard, "I am happy when I see that you have learned a cheerful patience."

"Are you?" Jerry replied, and smiled with childlike sweetness upon the old man. "Whisky, Don Manuel."

The host clapped his hands twice, and in haste two houseboys came running. "Whisky for Señor Peyton," said the Spaniard, "and in haste."

All the time that Jerry sat, looking into space, Don Manuel walked up and down the patio. He wore his long cloak, as usual, although the day was stifling hot; and when Jerry looked at the cadaverous face, pale as a lichen, he felt that there was truly no good warm blood in the body of the Don.

"A horse," Jerry said, for the hired horse on which he had ridden had been returned long since to the stables by one of Don Manuel's men.

Now the Spaniard clapped his hands again. "The bay gelding," the host ordered; whereat the man started and needed a second signal and a frown before he withdrew.

There was a long pause after that, with Jerry drinking steadily and alone, until four men came leading a bay horse. They led him as if he were a devil, and in truth Jerry saw a devil in the eye of the gelding. He rose and grinned once at his host; Don Manuel bowed, and Jerry vaulted into the saddle.

There followed a terrible five minutes in which the bay became a bolt of red fire, twisting into such odd shapes as only fire can assume, shaking himself from knot to knot. Most of the time he was in the air, and when he struck the earth it was only to jar it and spring aloft again. At the end of the five minutes he dropped his tail, put up his head, and cantered softly down the hill. A chorus of silence followed him from the servants and from Don Manuel; but Jerry rode straight on. The whisky was sending a genial warmth through his brain and heart, and there was a singular tingling in his finger tips. Jerry recognized that sensation, from old habit, as the signal of an approaching storm.

He rode straight across the island to the town of St. Hilaire to the house of the consul. It was nearly noon, but that gentleman was not yet up. Jerry moved two servants from the door and entered.

"Hello!" greeted the consul, after being lifted through the air and replaced on his bed. "What the devil?"

"Jeremiah Peyton," said the other.

The consul rubbed his other eye open.

"You must have a pretty bad town here," said Jerry.

"Why?" the consul inquired.

"They give you work that keeps you up all night," said Jerry with sympathy. He bound a wet towel around the author's head.

The consul found himself able to see, and therefore leaned out the window and gasped for breath. Presently he stood up again.

"Isn't that Don Manuel's Lightning that I see down there in the street?"

"No, that's my horse."

"Good heavens," said the consul, clasping his head, which seemed to reel with a thought, "did you ride him here?"

"I asked you about the town," Jerry replied. "How bad is it—to keep you up all night?"

"It isn't so bad," and the consul smiled. "I'm glad to see you riding Don Manuel's horse. How are things going?"

"Fair."

"Climbed any` fences? Busted through any?"

"No; I'm diggin' under one, though. About this town—"

"It's a quiet place," and again the consul sighed. "But I ran into a bunch of Irishmen last night; I wanted to go home, but they wanted to stay out. I didn't feel like hurting their feelings. You know?"

"Sure," Jerry agreed. "How many are there? I like Irishmen."

"Three," said the consul. "They're at the hotel. They have some Irish whisky, too."

"Only three?" said Jerry sadly. "What do they look like?"

"Their names are Sweeney, Murphy, and Smythe," the consul replied. "They're all over six feet and built right. Why do you ask?"

"You'll hear later," Jerry retorted, and went on his way.

Later he stood at a door of the hotel.

"Are you Sweeney, Murphy, or Smythe?" said Jerry.

"Maybe I'm all three," said the black-headed man at the door.

"Maybe you ain't," Jerry remarked.

"What the devil is it to you?" asked the black-headed man.

"I've just come from the consul," said Jerry, "and he says you're three fellows—with good whisky."

The black-headed man did not hear the last part of the sentence. He reached swiftly through the door and dragged Jerry into the room by the nape of the neck; and when he was fairly inside he spoke. "Now, son, talk sharp. Who told you you were a man?"

"My mama told me," said Jerry, and smote him upon the root of the nose.

Two large men in pajamas rose on either side of the room out of their beds and watched the fight.

Afterward they laid out the black-headed man on the

carpet and fell upon Jerry from both sides. The tingle had left the tips of his fingers and was in his shoulders. He hit hard and fast to get it out of him.

Finally he sat on a table, looking at his knuckles, which were raw.

"Who told you to come here?" queried the black-headed man, sitting up suddenly on the carpet.

"The consul," said Jerry.

"Oh," the black-headed man ejaculated. "I had an idea that he moved in the best circles." Then he added: "Why don't you have a drink?"

"I was waiting for you to pour it," said Jerry.

"Lift my friends off me," the black-headed man requested, for Jerry had made a heap of the three.

Jerry made a way for the black-headed man.

"Are you feeling better?" asked the Irishman.

"Lots."

"It's this climate," commented the Irishman. "It makes a man nervous in the fists. Here's to you!"

21

That day was a joyous oblivion, at the end of which Lightning carried Jerry softly and safely out to the house of Don Manuel. The don came out and superintended while three of his boys carried Jerry into the house and put him to bed. Afterward he sat up all night beside the bed, listening to Jerry snore. At the first coming of gray light he wakened his guest. "It's the third morning," said Don Manuel. "Get up."

Jerry rose like a lark, singing. "She's going to come," he said to Don Manuel.

"I know," the Spaniard replied. "I was twenty, once."

Jerry had hardly reached the top of the hill when he saw her come riding around the point of the beach and he ran down to meet her. He stood panting and holding her hand while he said: "It's taken three days to get you back, but it's worth the wait."

Then he saw that she was not in a bathing suit, but

was dressed formally for riding, with shining leather boots and trousers and a derby hat. There was only one touch of color, and that was a crimson blossom at her waist.

"You were seen in St. Hilaire yesterday," said the girl coldly.

"It's a fine little town, isn't it?"

"I suppose what's left of it is," she observed.

"I was killing time until you came again," explained Jerry.

"H-m-m," said Patricia, but her smile was irresistible.

"Why aren't you going to swim this mornin'?" asked Jerry.

"Because I have a sore foot," answered Patricia gloomily. She stared accusingly at him. "I cut it on a piece of coral at the other beach yesterday."

"Yep. None of the other beaches are any good."

She remembered something, and said, flushing: "Were you so sure I'd come back?"

"I knew you couldn't stand the mud and the coral rocks," said Jerry. "Won't you get off your horse?"

"I have to go right on," said Patricia.

"We could walk the horse the way you're going. It would rest him; besides, he looks sort of winded."

She glanced sharply at him, but he was looking only at the horse. "All right," said Patricia, and got down from the saddle. First she scanned all the hilltops swiftly.

"Are they following you?" asked Jerry.

"Why?"

"To find out if you see me."

"Do you think I've come out this morning just to see you?"

"Sure," said Jerry. "Take my arm."

The sand was deep, and she took his arm, but it was only to steady herself until she could find the right thing to say. "I think you'd better leave St. Hilaire," she said.

"I'm going to," Jerry replied.

"Aren't you happy here?" asked Patricia suddenly, unreasonably.

"Are you?" asked Jerry.

"Why do you say that?"

"You have big shadows under your eyes. You haven't been sleeping."

"Insomnia is an old trouble of mine," answered the girl, watching him. She sighed when he did not look back.

"I'm glad your foot doesn't bother you in the sand," said Jerry.

"There's a bandage on it," Patricia said instantly.

"Let's stop walking."

"Why?" But she paused with him.

"I'll tell you; the crunching on the sand starts to breaking in on what I think."

"They must be light thoughts," the girl commented idly.

"They're still thoughts," said Jerry, lowering his voice.

"Go on," Patricia urged.

"It's not a story I'm telling," Jerry replied, frowning. He began to look straight into her eyes.

"I have to go home," said Patricia suddenly.

"You don't."

"How do you know?"

"The sun isn't up."

Patricia swallowed. "You can't dictate, you know," she said.

"I'm studying up, though," answered Jerry.

"What d'you mean?"

"Why are you afraid?" asked Jerry in return.

"I'm not afraid."

"You look pretty white."

All at once she was leaning back against the shoulders of the cream-colored horse, and he turned his head and looked at her with his big, bright eyes.

"I'm unhappy," said Patricia, with her gloved hand at her breast.

It was a glove of some rough, soft leather; at the wrist wrinkled into many folds, and it was loose over the hand. It fascinated Jerry; he pored over it with a sort of sad delight. For one thing, it was a deep yellow, and the color seemed to him pleasant next to the crimson blossom.

"Is it connected up with me?" asked Jerry.

"I don't know," said Patricia.

"Are you kind of hollow inside?" inquired Jerry.

"Yes. How do you know?"

"Is it something like seasickness?"

"Yes, but worse; it—it stays with me."

"I know," said Jerry.

"What'll I do?"

"I tried whisky. I don't know what you'll do," he said more thoughtful than ever. "I feel the same way. I'll tell you something. I thought that when I saw you again I'd be a lot better right away, but I'm worse."

"I thought it was this beach," said Patricia. "I'm so used to seeing the sunrise here."

"But it isn't?"

"It isn't," said Patricia.

They stood close, looking miserably at each other.

"I'm never to see you again," said Patricia.

"That's your dad's work."

"He'll send me away from St. Hilaire if he ever finds out that I saw you again."

"Doesn't like me, does he?"

"I think he's afraid of you," she said slowly. "He was never afraid of any other man I ever heard of."

"Well, if you leave, I'll leave, too."

"Would you follow me?"

"Of course."

"It wouldn't do any good. If you followed me, dad would do you harm."

"Does he tell you why he hates me?"

"He says I couldn't understand."

There was another silence. A gull screamed far away, and the wind blew the sound lazily down to them.

"Will you come out here once in a while?" said Jerry.

"If I can. Suppose dad has seen me here?"

"But you'll come?"

"Yes."

"Shake on that."

He took her gloved hand; at the touch, something leaped from his heart to his brain and cast a mist across his eyes. Vaguely, he saw that her eyes were wide and that her lips were parted.

"It's a bargain now," said Jerry.

"Of course."

"You have to come, you see."

"I'll come. The sun is rising, Jerry."

"Good-by."

He helped her into the saddle.

"Wait a minute," said Jerry.

"Why?"

"Keep on looking out to sea. I'll tell you later."

She smiled faintly, and then looked out to sea.

"All right," said Jerry. "You can go now."

"What was it? Why did you make me do that?"

"I saw the sunrise hit your face. It made you look pretty fine."

"Oh, Jerry!"

"What's the matter?"

"Good-by!"

He stood back, dazed, and saw her whip the cream-colored horse. The animal switched his tail in protest, and then sprang away down the beach.

Jerry watched her out of sight and then went up the hillside more moodily than ever.

"Well?" asked the Spaniard, on the hilltop.

"Were you here all the time?"

"Of course, my son."

"Listen to me, partner. In your religion you go to a priest once in a while and get a lot of things off your chest, don't you?"

"Of course there is the confession."

"H-m-m," said Jerry. "And you don't particularly encourage other gents to hang around at that time?"

"There must be no third man there, of course."

"Well, keep away from this beach round about sunrise, Don Manuel, will you?"

"Ah," said Señor Guzman.

22

A messenger came to the house of Don Manuel that day before noon and brought a little envelope addressed in a feminine small hand to Mr. Jeremiah Peyton. Jerry opened it and read as follows:

My Dear Mr. Peyton:
You will be delighted to learn that I have at last come to agree with your viewpoint; and, if you will, I shall meet you on the beach, below the point which bounds the beach of Don Manuel, this evening after moonrise. There is a full moon, and the light should be pleasant, since we have no reading to do.

James P. Langley

All the letters were formed with a very fine line, and drawn out with the most exquisite precision. One felt a certain mechanical perfection, looking at this letter. It was rather like a printed form. Jerry held it close to his eyes, and still he could not see a waver or a scratch.

"A steady hand," said Jerry, and went to his room.

He remained there all day. He felt that he must bring his gun to the point of absolute perfection, and therefore he took it completely apart, oiled and cleaned it, and oiled it again with so delicate a film that it left the tip of the finger clean when one touched the mechanism. The trigger had grown stiff, and he lightened the pull.

Then he went through his regular routine of exercise—it had been three days since he had performed, and he found himself stale and rusty. It was not until the nerves along his arm would jump like a twist of lightning that he was content. All the time Don Manuel was walking up and down upon the hilltop, outside the window, a gaunt and ominous form.

Later on, Jerry went out and joined him. They did not speak a word for an hour, but each read the mind of the other. Jerry had a very small dinner, for, as Hank Peyton used to say, "a full stomach makes a slow hand," and when there was a pale semicircle of light over the eastern sea, Jerry said good-by to his host and went down from the hill to the beach.

He was in time, on rounding the point of the beach, to see a stream of silver come from the east across the ocean, which was very still; that light, at the same instant, picked a figure out of the gloom in front of Jerry, made the beach all white, and set the shadow of the figure walking over the white sand; a solitary gull wavered low down against the sky.

"You are in perfect accord with me," said the dispassionate voice of Langley.

"Thanks," said Jerry.

The other paused at a distance of some ten paces. "Am I too close?"

"Makes no difference to me," said Jerry cheerfully. "Close or far off."

"Before we begin," Langley said courteously, "I wish to compliment you on your scheme. It worked beautifully, as you see." Jerry saw the gleam of the white teeth beneath the shadow of the mustache. "The girl is under twenty and she has less sense than I thought."

"Are you done talking about her?" asked Jerry coldly.

"Certainly."

"Begin."

"Suppose," said Langley, "that in order to get a perfectly even start—"

"By all means," Jerry replied.

"We stand with our arms folded, then. We wait, say, for the next scream of the gull, and then both go for our guns. Is that satisfactory?"

"Excellent."

They stood rigid, their arms crossed, their shadows lying long and stiff on the white beach. Once a bird called from the inland; but neither of them stirred. Then came the cry of the gull. The bird had changed its course, and shooting straight over toward the land, it uttered a clear cry, hoarse as a sea wind; and the shadows on the beach leaped into action.

The arm of Langley shot straight out, for his gun had been worn under his coat, and in folding his arms he had simply settled his fingers about the butt. He flung his arm out, and the revolver exploded; but in the surety of the first shot, or because his arm swung too wide with its impetus, the bullet missed—it merely shaved through the coat of Jerry beneath the armpit as his right arm darted down and came up again, with a flash of metal.

Before the finger of Langley could press his trigger the second time the gun in Jerry's hand spoke. There was a loud clang as it struck metal, then a brief arch of light as the revolver was torn from the hand of the older man and flung away. He leaped after it with a moan of anxiety; but when he scooped it up, he saw Jerry standing with his own weapon hanging at his side.

"I'm sorry I didn't get you the first time," Jerry said calmly. "I can't shoot again."

Langley came to him walking like a cat, so soft and so light.

"I ought to blow your head off while you stand there like a fool," he said. "But I'll give you another chance. The next call of the gull is the signal."

"The gull's gone," said Jerry. "Besides, this is the end of it."

"Are you yellow?" Langley asked with a curse.

"It's out of our hands," Jerry replied solemnly. "Don't you see, Langley? You miss me. You play a dirty trick, getting your gun in your hand before the signal comes—even then you miss me, and I gather it's about the first time in your life that you've done such poor work. I sent my slug right down the alley and—it hits your gun. It knocks it out of your hand without even breaking the skin. Can you understand that?"

"I understand that you're backing down," the other replied. Jerry could see the heavy mustache bristling.

"You aren't cut out to be my meat," said Jerry calmly. "You aren't my size, pardner."

Langley stood without answer. His anger was making him pant.

"You're fat in the arm and fat in the head," went on Jerry, "and you can't stand up to me. Look me in the eye, Langley, and admit it!"

"We stay here," said the other, "till one of us is drilled."

"Go home, Langley. I can't pull a gun on you again."

The older man began to work at his throat. He seemed to be stifling.

"I don't know why I don't shoot you without argument," he said.

"You're a good deal of a dog," Jerry remarked calmly, "but you can't quite do that. Worse luck for you, Langley."

"You refuse to fight, then?" said Langley.

"I was set for the draw," said Jerry. "I'd have smiled if I drilled you the first shot, partner; if I pulled my gun again, I'd be shooting her father. Is that straight in your head? I'd be murdering her father because I know you haven't a chance."

"Is it possible?" cried Langley. "Am I listening to this and doing nothing?"

"I can't fight you," said Jerry, "so you've got a right over me. I'll give you my word not to see Patricia again."

"Your word?" said Langley eagerly. "Jerry, there's a touch of sound, clean sense in you!"

"Keep away!" said Jerry. "Stand off from me! I'll not see her until I've got rid of your objections. Good night."

"Nothing but a bullet will get rid of them," called Langley.

Don Manuel saw him come in, and when Jerry went by, the Spaniard shrugged his shoulders and sat down again, as one prepared for a long wait. But Jerry went to his room and wrote to Sheriff Edward Sturgis, at Sloan.

Dear Ed:

I'm here at the other end of the world, pretty near; and I suppose you're glad to have me here. I don't know how long I'll stick here; I'm at the end of a trail, you see, but a new one may begin most any day.

I'm writing this to ask a favor of you. You know most of the old boys who used to make Sloan the center for their celebrating.

In those times did you ever hear of a fellow named J. P. Langley, middle-sized, with black hair and eyes? He talks like the East, but he walks like a Westerner, and he handles a gun like an old-timer. I've an idea that if you look back into your mind you might unearth a pretty sizable record for him, and if you do, I could use it.

The point is, he's grown proud lately, and somebody ought to remind him of his past. And I can tell by his eye that he has one.

He's fixed well down here. He has millions, they say, and his dugout looks like it. Also, he has a daughter.

Well, good-by, Ed. Here's wishing you better luck than you ever wished me.

And say, Ed, don't you owe me a favor because I lifted myself and a lot of trouble out of your county? Yours,

Jeremiah Peyton

23

The thing which bothered Jerry more than anything else during the next ten days, or so, was really the conduct of Don Manuel. He knew without a word being spoken about it, that Jerry had met Langley; he also knew that neither of them had been killed in that meeting; and yet Señor Guzman remained perfectly equable. He protested with something close to tears when Jerry declared his intention of leaving the house and going to the hotel in St. Hilaire; so Jerry stayed on. He was left almost entirely to his own devices.

In the silent household of Don Manuel he came and went when he pleased. The servants obeyed him with as much eagerness as they obeyed their master. And Jerry noted this singular fact, that no servant in the Guzman household accepted gifts. He used to think of this, and then remember the quarters he had tossed to the men at Langley's place. Indeed, if he had been a nervous wreck seeking absolute retirement, Don Manuel would have been giving him a perfect vacation and rest cure; but Jerry represented some hundred and eighty or ninety pounds of iron-hard muscle without a nerve in it, and the inactivity ate into him day by day.

For seven mornings he had risen and gone to the hilltop from which he could look down, before sunrise, on the beach. And for four mornings Patricia came regularly before sunrise and stayed there until the day was well begun. But Jerry never went down to her. By the very fact that she was allowed to come out in the morning he knew, with a melancholy pleasure, that her father was trusting in his own promise not to see the girl. But on the fifth, sixth, and seventh mornings she did not come at all; and finally Jerry gave up his trips.

It was ten days after the letter that Sheriff Edward Sturgis arrived. He came in as much of a hurry as if he had ridden barely five miles and must turn back as soon as his horse was breathed. He, at least, had made no change in costume to suit the change in climate. He had his ancient felt hat, his shapeless trousers, his remarkable sack of a coat, always unbuttoned, just as he had worn them in Sloan. And when Jerry saw the sheriff standing in the entrance to the patio, he was swept directly back to the little town. He had connected Edward Sturgis with the law so long that he immediately forgot all about the letter; indeed, it seemed quite impossible that the sheriff should have come in answer to any written appeal. So he said as he took the stubby hand of Sturgis: "What's the matter, Ed? Do they want me back in Sloan?"

"Nothin' particular," said the sheriff, and his bright little eyes surveyed every inch of Jerry in a split-second glance. "I ain't heard any special mournin' because you're away, Jerry."

The latter smiled faintly. "Come in and sit yourself down, Ed. I'm some glad to see you."

He led the way to one of the tables in the patio; at his direction, cold drinks and strong drinks were brought, while the sheriff sat back and fanned himself with his hat and looked admiringly about on the coolness and upon Jerry.

"Kind of to home here, ain't you?" he commented.

"Old Spaniard runs this dump," said Jerry, who had forgotten to wonder at his own relations with the Don. "He's a pal of mine. Sort of took me in when I blew down into these parts. But come out with it, Ed. What do you want me for?"

"I don't want you," said the sheriff gently. He finished a drink, and continued to look about him. "This is a rum place, Jerry."

"But if you don't want me, who does?" asked Jerry.

"Durned if I know," replied the sheriff frankly. "I don't know of anybody that hankers after you particular. Why?"

"You haven't come here to take me back?" Jerry inquired, sitting back in his chair with a sigh of relief.

"Certainly not, Bud." The sheriff grinned. "Nothin' pleases me more than to have you do your plantin' of dead men outside my hang-out. Well, I'm glad you're fixed comfortable."

He continued to fan himself, always looking about him. He was one of those men who discover interesting details no matter where they may be. And his shoulders were so humped with riding a horse and sitting at a desk that when he looked around he had to move his head in hitches, so to speak.

"Not bad," said Jerry, still looking narrowly at the sheriff. "I hope you're not trying to put something over on me, Ed."

"What makes you ask that?"

"I dunno," said Jerry. He leaned back in his chair again, with one hand behind his head, but his right hand was always free, always unemployed, with the fingertips continually tapping lightly on something. No matter in how perfect a state of quiescence he might be, that right hand remained alive, as though it were controlled by a separate intelligence. All of this the sheriff noted.

"You're always set for something, ain't you, Jerry?"

"That's where you're all wrong," said Jerry. "I'm never set—I'm just sort of expectin'."

"Oh, all right," and Sturgis grinned. "Put it that way, then."

"I'm glad you understand," Jerry said. "This is pretty peaceful country, but I believe in goin' prepared for war."

"Get that out of your head, Jerry. I'm not down here gunning for you. I'm pretty smooth, maybe, but I don't drink with a man I want to get."

"I know that, Ed. But tell me straight, hasn't your bein' down here got—"

"Got something to do with you? Well, maybe it has. Maybe it hasn't."

"Take your time," said Jerry. "I hate to rush a man. Have another drink. You weren't interested in what I wrote about Langley, were you?"

"I seen what you said about him."

"Know him?"

"I dunno. What's he look like? Oh, I remember you told me what he was like. Well, I'd like to look him over."

"I can't take you over to see him, Ed. Him and me, we had a little falling out. In a word, he's a skunk, Ed."

"You don't say," murmured the sheriff conversationally. He settled himself to hear a story.

"He must have millions," said Jerry. "But he made a flying trip up to Chambers City on some queer sort of business, and on the way he took it into his head that he wanted the Voice of La Paloma. Somebody must have told him about it while he was going through. Or else he was an old-timer in those parts and knew all about it already. Anyway, he stuck me up for it when I was helpless with my wrists all bunged up. I took his trail; and here I am. But the way he rode that country up home made me think he was an old-timer there; so I wrote to you to see if you knew his record."

"Have you met up with him?"

"Twice."

"And you're both still healthy—up and around?"

Jerry flushed.

"You must be kind of out of practice, Jerry."

"The first time he wouldn't pull his gun, Ed. The second time—well, I hit his gun with my slug the first shot and then—"

"Well?"

"I dunno. We just sort of parted, Ed."

"Is he good?"

"Fastest I ever saw. But he tried a crooked stunt. It spoiled his aim. That's why I'm here chinning with you."

"For a boy," said Sturgis, "you're a cool kid. I sort of like you, Jerry. What about this girl?"

The question came so suddenly that Jerry winced. "What girl?" he said.

"The one you talked about in your letter."

"What did I say in the letter?" inquired Jerry, dazed.

"That you were out of your head about Langley's daughter.

"Did I say that? I thought—well, I can't answer you, Ed."

"The girl spoiled your play with Langley, is that it?" asked the sheriff.

"How d'you mean?"

"What's she like?" asked the sheriff suddenly.

"You mean what does she look like?"

"Yep."

Jerry raised his head and studied the adobe wall. His restless right hand was still, the sheriff noted.

"Suppose," said Jerry, "that you been on a party and your head is hot, and your mouth full of ashes—well, you step out into the morning and a cool wind hits your face—"

"Is she like that?" the sheriff inquired.

But Jerry was still absentmindedly studying the wall. "Suppose you been riding the desert," he went on slowly, "and you drop out of the mountains into a valley full of fruit trees, and spring; and you ride along with the blossoms dropping around you; and the birds fightin' in the tops of the trees and—"

"Is she like that?" asked the sheriff with increasing emphasis.

"Suppose," said Jerry, "that you been playing poker, and the luck's against you, and you step out into the night and look up and see how still the sky is with all the stars close down—"

"Oh, Lord," the sheriff exclaimed without heat.

"What's the matter?" said Jerry, looking dazed again.

"Do you see much of her?"

"Her father's against her seeing me, you know."

"So—"

"She came down for a while where we used to meet.

But I couldn't fight it out with the old boy—he's her father. Put a mist over his eyes and they're about the same as her eyes, see.

"H-m-m!" said the sheriff.

"I couldn't fight it out with him, so I didn't have any right to go sneaking around seeing his daughter. So I promised him that I wouldn't talk to her any more."

The sheriff started violently. Jerry looked at him in surprise, but the sheriff was only crossing his legs, which was a considerable feat, owing to the size of his stomach and the shortness of the legs.

"Well, Ed, the odds were sort of against me. I think he's a crook. But I have no proof. I want to be able to go around and talk straight to him. I want to be able to say: 'I haven't a cent and I've been a rough one, but I've been clean. You've got a fortune, but you're crooked. What you say about your daughter doesn't make the slightest difference to me!' "

"I follow you," said the sheriff. He added with his characteristic suddenness: "Does the girl miss you, Jerry?"

"I don't know, Ed."

"She came down to your meeting place even after you'd stopped going there?"

"That doesn't mean anything. She likes to see the sun rise there."

"H-m-m," said the sheriff. "Well, I don't suppose you could introduce me to this Langley?"

"Not without a troop of cavalry, Ed."

"I'm going out to look him over."

"I'll show you his house."

"You needn't mind. I located that before I came to see you.

"Come back here for the night, Ed. Don Manuel will

be glad to see you. Particularly if you know anything about Langley's past. He's interested, too."

"Come back here?" echoed the sheriff vaguely. "Oh, yes. Sure. Good-by, Jerry."

24

Langley was a strong believer in efficiency, and he knew that efficiency means a concentration of the executive authority in anything from a nation to a household. And therefore, shortly after their honeymoon ended, when his wife began a sentence with "I think—" he promptly answered: "My dear, you're much too nice to waste your pleasantness thinking. Hereafter I'll do your thinking for you."

Mrs. Langley was one of those calm-eyed women who know how to look the truth in the face and smile. She saw her husband for the first time, really, but she smiled when she heard him say this. After that she was never known to rebel against fate, and the word of Langley was fate in his household.

Only of late, as Patricia grew into womanhood, there had been vague stirrings of revolt behind the calm eyes of her mother; and on this evening the storm broke suddenly and without warning on the head of the rich man. Mrs. Langley had placed herself between him and the door and lifted her head and told him that, whether he willed it or not, her daughter was to be happy.

"And will you tell me," Langley replied, "what I'm grinding my heart out for if it isn't her happiness?"

"She's been in her room—and hardly out of it—for forty-eight hours," said Mrs. Langley.

"She's sick?" Langley asked, changing color.

"The doctor told you that."

"Fever," said Langley. "Nothing unusual at this season."

"The doctor is a fool." It was a strong word for her. It made even J. P. Langley stop—mentally—and look at her again. He had known long ago that she had little tenderness for him, but he had been content with knowing that he controlled her. Also she was decorative and knew how to make his guests happy; so that it came to him with a distinct shock, as he looked at her this evening, and discovered that she was very close to hating him. "The doctor is a fool," repeated his wife, as though she feared he had not heard.

"He is the best in St. Hilaire."

"She has a fever," said Mrs. Langley, "but it's a fever of longing, James!" She made a little gesture with her palm up, but Langley was thinking so hard and fast that he did not notice. It was a gross error, for when her hand fell back to her side it gathered into what was almost a fist. "She's in love," she added coldly.

"Give her quinine just the same," said Langley. "Give her quinine and rest. That'll do the work."

"Do you really intend to make her marry where you wish?" asked Mrs. Langley calmly.

"Of course I do. Good heavens, Mary, are you surprised by that?"

"And yet," she pursued, more to herself than to him, "she's more your child than she is mine." She added: "I think you're breaking her heart, James."

"Not in this century," and Langley chuckled. "They may be strained, but they don't break. It's out of date."

"Ah!" said his wife, and smiled to herself. It was growing to be a habit of hers, this inward smile, and it always maddened Langley. He stood rubbing his mustache, and smiling in jerks.

"There's one trouble with you, my dear," he said. "Ever since the first baby died—"

"James!" she cried faintly.

"I've got to say it," he persisted. "Ever since that, you've an idea that every man is a baby. By heavens, I think you're fond of this infernal snake in the grass without ever having seen him."

"I like what Patricia tells me about him. He has an honest way of talking."

"What makes you think that?"

"Because it's just a little foolish. She's told me all the silly things he's said at least ten times over. She sees nothing funny in them, James."

"This ends it," he said angrily. "I forbid you to talk to her about him, Mary."

"It's impossible for me to obey you," his wife replied.

He tried to speak, but could not. "Do you mean that?" he managed to say at last.

"Yes."

He jerked open the door and fled, for he was in a panic, and the thing he feared was himself. As he went downstairs, every servant he passed was a blow. He hated their faces, and to escape them he fled into the night, down the road, and twisted off onto a bypath until he stood in a place where the evening light filtered softly and coolly about him. There he stood still, and tried to arrange his thoughts.

"Pat," called a voice, and the sheriff stepped out. "You're losing the old quick eye," the sheriff said. "I made as much noise as a herd of yearlings in stubble, but you never heard me."

"What in the name of the devil are you doing here?"

"I've come down to see the other end of the joke I played on you in Sloan. Seems to have worked out, all right."

"I'll send your man back to you wrapped up in wood before he's a month older," Langley retorted. "I'd have done it long ago, but he refused to fight. Yellow!"

"Mostly," said the sheriff, "you lie well. But now you're mad. Going back to that joke—"

"Confound you, Sturgis."

"Now, now," said the sheriff soothingly. "Ain't he a rough talker! I guess Jerry has sort of irritated you, Pat."

"I'll give you two minutes to talk sense and get out."

"That's plenty. I'll tell you, Pat. When I sicked Jerry onto you in Sloan, I sort of thought I was usin' one useless gent to wipe out another. Then I got a letter that made me think maybe I was wastin' a man's life to kill a snake, you bein' the snake. Back in Sloan I thought Jerry was just a public danger. Now I c'n see he's just young. And all he needed was somethin' to tie to. Can you beat the bad luck that makes him tie to your daughter?"

"Is that bug in your fool head, too?"

"You ain't even got a sense of humor left, have you, Pat?" said the sheriff, wondering. "Funny thing, I figure. When a man's crooked it's a sort of cancer. It starts with a little thing and eats all the good right out of him."

"I can't listen to your chatter anymore, Sturgis. Finish and get off the place. I can't waste time on you here."

"So," went on the sheriff calmly, "I figured it this way: I'll go down and see what the boy amounts to now. I come, and what d'you think? Jerry's in love with your kid. Well, Pat, nothin' but a man-sized man can be in love with a girl the way he is with her. Now, it wouldn't be right to throw him away to kill a skunk. No, it wouldn't. I seen that. But look at me. You busted me up twenty years ago. I been just driftin' along, mostly no good. And now I see it's my job."

"Ah," said Langley, "I begin to understand. You've come and brought your gun, eh? You really think you can beat me to the draw, Ed?" He smiled almost in friendship on the sheriff.

"No," Sturgis went on. "I know you're faster and straighter. But always before, I been figurin' on gettin' in the first shot and then comin' away clean of hurt. Now I see that my one chance to get you, Pat, is to soak up about three of your slugs while I plant one in your innards. Is that straight?

"So you're going to clean up, Ed?"

"I sure am, Pat."

"When I had that affair with your girl twenty years ago, I had an idea that it would end this way—I'd have to wipe you off the slate. Yet in a way, Ed, I hate to do it, because—"

He had extended his left hand as he spoke, and now he raised his right hand. It came past his waistline carrying a revolver, and the explosion tore off the end of his last word. Flinching from that glint of metal, the sheriff had turned, drawing his own gun; so that the

slug struck him across the chest and the weight of it
toppled him to the ground. He would have fallen
prone, helpless, had he not struck a tree trunk as he
fell, and he slid in a bunch to the ground. He began
raising his revolver.

As for Langley, he had paused to observe the effect
of his shot, and now he drove in another. It was meant
for the forehead of the sheriff, but at that moment he
drew his head back with a jerk, and the bullet crashed
down through his breast. It sent a quiver through the
sheriff, as though he shook with cold. His face seemed
already dead, and his mouth was hanging wide, but the
muzzle of his revolver tilted and pointed up, and as
Langley fired for the third time, the sheriff's gun
exploded, and the bullet struck Langley squarely between the eyes.

Afterward the sheriff lived long enough to crawl over
to the fallen body.

"A good-lookin' man like him" said the sheriff, "had
ought to make a good-lookin' stiff."

So he took the arms of Langley and folded them
across his breast. And he closed the eyelids, and the
open, horrified mouth.

"Now," said the sheriff, "I'll tell a man that was worth
doin'. It makes him a picture."

He put his own back against the tree. Presently he
felt his right hand growing cold, and looking down, he
saw the revolver which he had never dropped from his
fingers.

"Well, well," said the sheriff, "the Voice of La Paloma
come in for the last word, after all!"

25

It was a long time after this. The United States consul of St. Hilaire sat on the front porch and three Irishmen sat around him. They had been drinking for some time, and there was still liquor before them. They had passed the stage of hilarity; they had reached the stage of solemnity. The consul had just finished a story and he was telling them about it.

"You see that boat?" he said.

A long, low, graceful white launch of comfortable width was sliding up the bay. There happened to be no other boats in the bay except fishing smacks, tilting this way and that as they tacked to port; the wind was coming out from the land, and yet it allowed the murmur of the white boat's engine to come distinctly to the house of the consul.

"That, in fact," said the consul, "is him now."

The three Irishmen did three things. After standing

up, one of them raised his hand to his nose, another touched an eye, the third caressed the angle of his jaw. They looked and looked until the yacht was far down the bay.

"That was Jerry standing on the poop," they said in one voice. "And was that his wife?"

"Sure."

"Well, then, Patricia's gone!" said the three Irishmen, and sighed. "It ought to be a good yarn," they added, turning to the consul.

"It's a good story," he admitted, "but there's a missing link. I still don't know whether he climbed the fence or busted it or mined it."

The three Irishmen made each their peculiar gestures.

"He probably used all the ways," they said. "He couldn't do three things at once fairly well."

The Best of Adventure
by RAMSAY THORNE

5 EXCITING ADVENTURE SERIES
MEN OF ACTION BOOKS

___**NINJA MASTER**
by Wade Barker
Committed to avenging injustice, Brett Wallace uses the ancient
Japanese art of killing as he stalks the evildoers of the world in his
mission.
___**#7 SKIN SWINDLE**   *(C30-227, $1.95)*
___**#8 ONLY THE GOOD DIE**   *(C30-239, $2.25, U.S.A.)*
                                 (C30-695, $2.95, Canada)

___**THE HOOK**
by Brad Latham
Gentleman detective, boxing legend, man-about-town, The Hook
crossed 1930's America and Europe in pursuit of perpetrators of insur-
ance fraud.
___**#1 THE GILDED CANARY**   *(C90-882, $1.95)*
___**#2 SIGHT UNSEEN**   *(C90-841, $1.95)*
___**#5 CORPSES IN THE CELLAR**   *(C90-985, $1.95)*

___**S-COM**
by Steve White
High adventure with the most effective and notorious band of military
mercenaries the world has known—four men and one woman with a
perfect track record.
___**#3 THE BATTLE IN BOTSWANA**   *(C30-134, $1.95)*
___**#5 KING OF KINGSTON**   *(C30-133, $1.95)*

___**BEN SLAYTON: T-MAN**
by Buck Sanders
Based on actual experiences, America's most secret law-enforcement
agent—the troubleshooter of the Treasury Department—combats the
enemies of national security.
___**#1 A CLEAR AND PRESENT DANGER**   *(C30-020, $1.95)*
___**#2 STAR OF EGYPT**   *(C30-017, $1.95)*
___**#3 THE TRAIL OF THE TWISTED CROSS** *(C30-131, $1.95)*
___**#5 BAYOU BRIGADE**   *(C30-200, $1.95)*

___**BOXER UNIT—OSS**
by Ned Cort
The elite 4-man commando unit of the Office of Strategic Studies whose
dare-devil missions during World War II place them in the vanguard of the
action.
___**#3 OPERATION COUNTER-SCORCH** *(C30-128, $1.95)*
___**#4 TARGET NORWAY**   *(C30-121, $1.95)*

"THE KING OF THE WESTERN NOVEL" IS *MAX BRAND*